THE RACE

THE RACE
CAROL MATAS

HarperCollins*PublishersLtd*

First Edition

Canadian Cataloguing in Publication Data

Matas, Carol, 1949—
    The race

ISBN 0-00-223743-1

I. Title.

PS8576.M37R33 1991   C813'.54   C91-094736-8
PR9199.3.M37R33 1991

---

91 92 93 94 95 RRD 5 4 3 2 1

Dedication

For my sister Susan and my brother John, who know
what it is to grow up in a political household. And for
Robert and Stephanie.

Acknowledgements

The author wishes to thank all those who took time from their hectic political schedules to give her interviews. She also wishes to thank the Manitoba Arts Council for its financial support.

THE RACE

ITINERARY

TUESDAY, JULY 5

11 A.M.	Arrive in Calgary
P.M.	Registration

WEDNESDAY, JULY 6

10 A.M.	Young Liberals of Canada Biennial Meeting
12 A.M.	Forum with Leadership Candidates sponsored by Young Liberals of Canada
3 P.M.	Meeting at Green House followed by campaigning
7 P.M.-9 P.M.	Forum with Leadership Candidates sponsored by Women's Commission
9:30 P.M.-1 A.M.	Young Liberals of Canada social

THURSDAY, JULY 7

7:30 A.M.-9:30 A.M.	Pancake breakfast
9:30 A.M.	Meeting at Green House with Winnipeg South Youth
10 A.M.-11:30 A.M.	Opening ceremonies
P.M.	Party business (you need not attend)
5 P.M.	Barbecue at Hotel with Mom
7 P.M.	Tribute to Croix
8:30 P.M.	Rodeo and dance

FRIDAY, JULY 8

10:30 A.M.	Winnipeg South Youth meeting, Green House
11 A.M.-12:30 A.M.	Forum with leadership candidates sponsored by Aboriginal Commission (Roundup Centre)
P.M.	Pre-speech preparations with Winnipeg South Youth
6 P.M.-8:30 P.M.	Demonstrations and speeches (Saddledome)
9 P.M.-1 A.M.	Dance at Roundup Centre

SATURDAY, JULY 9

9 A.M.	Winnipeg South Youth meet at Green House
10 P.M.	Delegate canvassing
P.M.	Voting, speeches, reception in Roundup Centre

DAY 1

TUESDAY, JULY 5

11 A.M.

The wheels touch down on the tarmac, sending a jolt through my body. I realize I am clutching the armrests.

"White knuckles," Lara teases.

I follow her gaze and realize she's right. I slowly loosen my grip and give her a sheepish smile. But I know, and she knows, it's not just the landing that is making me nervous.

"It all seemed like such a good idea at the time," I say to her.

"Ali," she responds in her firm voice, "it *was* a good idea and it *is* a good idea."

I'm just glad Lara is here. She always gives my confidence a boost just when I really need it—which is usually every five minutes.

We gather our stuff—I have a knapsack and my jean jacket—and file off the plane. The minute we get off, we can tell we are in the city hosting a leadership convention.

Since it's Calgary everyone has on cowboy hats. Booths are set up to give direction to people. Volunteers from my mother's camp and others are running around making sure all the delegates get on the right bus. Everyone is wearing buttons for the candidate they support. Mom's colours are green on a Liberal red background—green for our name, Green. I think the combination is simply horrible, but it does catch your eye. James's colours are red and white, Heraux's yellow and white, Potter's are blue and white and Baker's are black and white.

The airport is a mass of chaos. You can feel the excitement in the air, though. Everyone is greeting friends who are coming off other flights, calling to people, waving, chattering.

"Stay here and grab our bags," Lara yells at me over the hubbub. "I'll go see if I can find our bus."

I have to muscle my way to the edge of the roundabout to pick up our bags. I accidentally land Lara's, which is really large, on the foot of the guy standing beside me.

"Oh," I exclaim, "I'm sorry." I look up and see that it's a kid wearing a James button. He takes another out of his pocket and offers it to me as he extracts his foot from under the bag.

"Wear this and make it up to me," he smiles.

Boy, is he cool. He's tall, almost six feet I bet, and he's got blond hair, real short on one side, with long bangs on the other falling into his eyes. His eyes are blue and he doesn't have a pimple on his face. Unlike me. I had a major break-out this morning and am growing a zit that will soon rival the Rockies in size. Right in the middle of my chin. I find my hand covering it before I can stop myself.

"No thanks," I mumble. "But sorry about your foot."

"My foot? Oh my foot!" He pauses. "Maybe it's broken." He feigns pain. "Maybe I'll have to miss this whole thing now. Oh no! You'll have to take my place. Take off that

4

button." He points to my Green button. "You'll have to take my place now."

I can't help but laugh even though he's being a real goof.

"I don't think so," I reply. I mean how should he know he's talking to the front runner's daughter?

"Ali, Ali!" I turn to see Lara waving to me. She hustles over, grabs her bag, which is on wheels—she's brought enough clothes for a month—and motions me to follow her. The shuttle is nowhere to be found but they've arranged a bus for us all.

"Let's go."

I pick up my black nylon bag, filled mostly with cut-off jeans and T-shirts. I have to take my hand away from my chin to do it.

"Bye!" The goof waves. "See you 'round."

"Yeah, bye," I answer as I follow Lara.

"So, the two of you meet so soon, eh?" Lara says to me as we settle into the seats of the bus.

"I dropped your bag on his foot, that's all."

Lara laughs.

"Good thing he didn't think you did it on purpose."

I'm not following her at all. "What do you mean?"

"That's Alexander James's son, Paul," she smiles.

Wow. And I thought it was funny he was trying to convert me, 'cause he didn't know who I was!

"I don't suppose you broke his foot?" she asks, her voice almost wistful.

"Lara!" I say. "You're so bad. We'll beat his dad, no problem. And without maiming his family. Although," I add, "I'm sure I couldn't have found a better person to drop five hundred pounds on."

"I take offence at that!" Lara retorts. "My bag does not weigh five hundred pounds!"

Lara is my mom's executive assistant. She's twenty-four and has been working for my mom since she graduated in political science two years ago. To me she's kind of an aunt and best friend all in one.

"I hope we can beat his dad," she sighs. "It's too close for comfort, though. And Heraux is creeping up on us too."

Good, I think to myself. Maybe we won't have to move to Ottawa after all. And my secret hope is alive once more.

1 P.M.

I prop the pillows up on the bed and lean into them with a sigh of relief. Bliss. Peace and quiet for at least half an hour till Mom arrives. Lara is already next door in Mom's suite, organizing who knows what on the phone. I grab the TV remote and start flipping channels. Dad and Michael won't arrive until the big speeches on Friday because they're both working. Mike thinks he's so cool because he just turned eighteen, and he keeps saying to me, "Those of us who can vote, *and* drive *and* are in university . . ." Big deal. He has a job as a lifeguard and it's a good job, and that's part of the reason I'm here and he's not. He can't get off work till the weekend but I'm completely free this summer. He's really ticked off about it because he loves all this political stuff and doesn't want to miss a minute of it. And of course, I don't and here I am. Well, I have no one to blame but myself. Still, that thought doesn't make me feel an awful lot better. I can't

7

even stay in the hotel room if it all gets too boring. I got voted in as a delegate. So I have to go to everything.

I glance over the itinerary Lara has left lying open on my bed. Outside of today, which is just registration and stuff, the days are crammed full—and Lara's warned me that the itinerary is just the bare bones. All the delegates are expected to work every waking minute, and *sleep* is not a priority.

I think back to when Mom first ran for parliament, a little over three years ago. She was a lawyer so she's always worked, but this was different. Suddenly she was never home and we had a housekeeper doing all our cooking and cleaning because Dad was gone too, out campaigning with her. And every time I had a party or something on with my friends, I'd have to cancel because she'd need me to stand in some room for an hour waiting for her to finish speaking and then Mike and I would be brought out on stage like prize possessions to be shown off. Okay—maybe not every time. In fact that only happened three times but three times was enough! I almost died of embarrassment. And she'd make me wear a geeky dress because jeans and cut-offs just weren't "appropriate." And on the bus coming home from school kids would start chanting "Morin, Morin, Morin," because that was the name of Mom's opponent. Kids I didn't even know. What jerks. It was really embarrassing.

Even though she got so busy she still managed to be as overprotective as ever—phoning me every other minute to make sure I was doing my homework or I wasn't out too late. And she still managed to make sure I was the first kid picked up from a party on Saturday night—she'd get Mike to do her dirty work. I'd hoped she'd be too busy to notice what I was doing, but no such luck. It seems to me I got the worst deal possible—a mother who is never there when you want her but manages to be there when you don't want her!

If I wasn't busy with my friends (who aren't the *least* bit interested in any of this), then I'd help out sometimes at home. The worst was counting out pamphlets into piles of five hundred, stuffing them into envelopes, licking them shut, licking the stamps, then sticking on the names and addresses. After four hours of that, I had enough glue in my stomach to keep my guts stuck together for weeks. Ugh!

Sometimes I'd go out canvassing with Mom. Door to door. "Hello, I'm Rosaline Green and this is my daughter, Alison." Alison smiles sweetly. "I hope we can count on your support in the election."

Most people were pretty friendly, although we did meet a few Tories who were very rude, and some people from what Mom calls the "Cynics Party" who'd just say, "I hate all politicians. They're all the same. They're all out for themselves."

Well, I happen to know Mom isn't like that—I mean, she deserved to win. She's honest and smart and really cares about making Canada a better place to live, with good education and no poverty. Especially no homeless or hungry. She says she'll wipe out every food bank in the country and give people enough to live in dignity. She deserved to win then and she deserves to win now. But I'm not sure I want her to win this one.

I must admit, election night, almost three years ago, was really exciting. Rosaline Green, the new member of Parliament for Winnipeg South, now known as "our M.P." My mother would be representing all these people in Ottawa. What a party we had. I stayed up till four in the morning. We all did. Then Mom had to go to Ottawa to find an apartment and that's when it all sank in. She promised we wouldn't have to move and so she stays in Ottawa Monday through Thursday and comes home Friday to Sunday. But even when she's home in Winnipeg she's never actually there. I mean she has to meet with her constituents— the people in her riding—and she has all these functions to attend. She says it's very important to keep in touch with the people here so she can raise their concerns in Ottawa, in the House of Commons. The day I got my period, I had to phone Lara and ask *her* what to do. Mom certainly wasn't available for such minor details. I might have gotten more attention if I'd asked her to raise it as a question in the House. "Excuse me, Mr. Speaker, which brand of feminine protection do you recommend, and how do you use it?"

Of course there are a few good things. Like the trips. She's had me down to Ottawa quite a few times, a couple of times on my own, sometimes with Dad and Mike. It's only a one-bedroom place so Mike and I always bring our sleeping bags.

She took us on a private tour of the House of Commons. We ate in the fancy dining room, which was too fancy for me. There wasn't a decent thing on the menu—I had a salad. Later I went to the cafeteria—that has good food, burgers, fries, stuff like that. We went to the clock tower and she took us to meet M. Croix. As the Tories (or Conservatives) now form the government, M. Croix's official title is Head of the Opposition. As leader of the Liberal Party, with the second biggest majority in parliament, M. Croix's job is to criticize the government, point out their mistakes and suggest a better way of doing things. If my mother wins and replaces him, and the Liberals beat the Tories in the next election, she could be the first woman prime minister of Canada. Almost a year ago, Mom had explained that she'd be running for the Liberal leadership and that, of course, if she won we'd have to move.

After that there were even more demands made on my time than when she'd run for office the first time. I often had to be somewhere with her. Sometimes she would take three different flights a day, going from one city to another. Or she would drive day and night to tiny little gatherings where she'd meet Liberals and try to get their support. Sometimes I'd go with her. The flying made me a nervous wreck, the car trips made me car sick. And behind it all, I knew it meant we'd have to move to Ottawa if she won.

I'm shaken out of my reverie by a loud knock at the door. I know right away it's Mom. She has this kind of authority in her knock.

"It's me!" she calls.

I open the door. She gives me a peck on the cheek and bustles into the room. She looks around. Two double beds, a sofa and chair, big TV. The usual.

"Well, this is nice. How was your flight?"

"Good."

"Okay darling, I'm just next door if you need anything. We're having a meeting with the regional chairs in an hour and Lara has to brief me on things. You're welcome to sit in if you want."

She always says that. She means it, too. She thinks these meetings are so interesting that she's doing me a favour letting me sit in on them. She's always trying to include me. But they're *so* boring. I tried it once. That was enough.

"No thanks," I say. "I have to go over to the grounds and register. Lara thinks I should do it today because I'll probably have meetings tomorrow."

"How will you get there?" she asks.

"I'll take a cab. Lara gave me money."

Mom nods. "Well, all right. Let's meet back here at six for dinner, okay? Maybe there's a movie on pay TV you can watch tonight."

"Yeah, sure," I reply. "See you then."

She gives me another peck and she's gone. Lara already showed me Mom's suite. It's *big*. A huge living room and a kitchen, and a bedroom with a balcony, and two bathrooms, the one in the bedroom with a Jacuzzi.

I no sooner shut the door than Lara lets herself in with her key.

"I think I'll go with you." She smiles.

Mom has told her she does *not* want me going over to the convention grounds alone, in a taxi. Overprotective as usual.

"I need to register anyway." Lara grins. "Ready?"

"Yeah, sure," I say, relieved that Lara's going to go with me, although not for the same reasons as my mom. I don't want to get lost and wander around like an idiot. And what if I don't meet anyone I know?

"Then let's go. I have to get back for the meeting. I'll arrange for a volunteer to pick you up outside the Big Four later," she adds. "You can hang around the place until then."

"Fine," I sigh, not looking forward to being totally on my own.

The hotel lobby is a mass of people talking, laughing, most wearing red cowboy hats with the name Green emblazoned in—what else?—green across the front. There is also a huge group of journalists who are obviously waiting for Mom or someone, anyone, to interview. Lara slips past them, hails a cab, and in five minutes we're entering the Calgary Stampede grounds where the convention is to take place.

Calgary looks like a nice city. The mountains in the distance are so pretty and the air is really clean, just like in Winnipeg. It has lots more tall buildings than Winnipeg has but it doesn't seem all that different to me.

The stampede grounds are something else though. The

first thing I see is the Saddledome. It's huge and round and has what looks like train windows going all around its middle.

"Is that a subway?" I ask Lara.

She laughs and pokes me with her elbow. "No silly, it's just the design."

Well, how should I know? It looks very futuristic. We drive into the grounds until the cab stops in front of a big square building called the Big Four. I follow Lara and she follows the signs. We go into the basement where people are registering. The registration is done with amazing efficiency. In no time I've had my picture taken and been given a plastic ID. The ID is attached to a silver chain that you put over your head and wear so it hangs on your chest. Before putting it on I examine my picture. It is totally geeky—all you can see is metal because I made the mistake of smiling. Upper and lower braces. Black hair cut in a bob. Brown eyes. All my mother's friends say I'm beautiful but I know better. For one thing I'm too short. Just creeping up on five three. Mom is like that. Short. Actually Dad isn't and Mike isn't. Just my luck to get her height genes. Mom's black hair is super short and she has green eyes. Green. Too much.

"Hi there!"

I can feel myself blushing. I must've been studying my ID so hard I was oblivious to everything. I look up. It's the goof, what's his name? He's with a whole crowd of James kids. They're all wearing red baseball caps with James written across the front in white. I like the caps, they're cool. I'd much rather have one of those than a stupid cowboy hat.

"Decided to switch yet?" he asks.

I can see Lara is ready to do the big introduction. I don't know what makes me do it, but I push past her and him.

"Can't stop. Gotta run. See you." And I'm out of there.
Lara runs after me.

"What was all that about?"

I can feel my face is completely beet red.

"I don't know," I giggle. "I don't know why I did that. All of a sudden I just didn't want to be Rosaline Green's daughter."

Lara points to my ID card, which I am still clutching in my hand.

"It's there for everyone to read, hon." She smiles. "That won't work for long."

"No, I guess it won't. And now he thinks I'm a complete stupid idiot for running off that way."

We emerge onto the steps of the Big Four. "Look," Lara says, "we've rented that cabin over there for all the Green delegates; we're calling it Green House. Go there and check it out. And that building," she says, pointing to another one to the right of Green House, "is the Roundup Centre. It's where all our booths are and where all the meetings will be held for the next few days. Want to wander around? I can have a car right here for you at five."

"Sure," I agree. "Why not? But make it four. It'll be boring just walking around all afternoon."

"But you should go to Green House," Lara says. "All the delegates are supposed to go there to get their kits." She is already holding two carry bags full of paper—one for each of us—that we were given at the registration booth. They contain the timetable of events, and all sorts of brochures and info on the convention. "I'll take yours back to the hotel so you don't have to lug it around," she adds.

She hails a cab and takes off. I wander over to Green House. It's a beautiful day. The sky is blue, the temperature warm, and my spirits start to lift. Maybe this won't be so bad.

I think back to the moment when I announced I'd run as

14

a delegate. I wasn't even sure how all this delegate stuff worked. Lara explained it to me one night.

"Every Liberal riding association will elect twelve delegates to go to the leadership convention and represent them. Four men, four women, four youths—two male, two female between the ages of fourteen and twenty-five—and four alternates. We will run a slate of candidates who will state that if they are elected, they'll vote for your mom. The other candidates will also run slates. If we win, your mom will have twelve sure votes on election day at the leadership convention."

"Can they change their minds once they're at the convention?" I asked.

"Actually yes, but we hope that won't happen," Lara grinned. "Mike and I are going to run as youth delegates," she added.

"Yeah," I said, "well, maybe I will too!"

"Oh no, I don't think so, dear," Mom butted in. I thought she was deep into a book and not listening at all.

"Why not?" I said. (I'd really just been joking. I mean, I did *not* want to run for anything. It would be too embarrassing.)

"Well, there are so many people who have worked so hard for me, dear. We want to give them a chance to run. Otherwise they have to pay five hundred dollars to go as observers *and* they don't get to vote. They also have to pay for their air fare and hotel, so it can get expensive."

I don't know what came over me—I really don't— but I heard myself say, "And I suppose I haven't worked hard for you? I don't deserve it?"

"No, dear, it's not that, but fourteen is very young. Most of the youth delegates will be older and they'll have worked longer and harder than you."

"Fine," I said. "Don't put me on your slate. But I'm going to run. And I'm going to win."

My mom just smiled. She knows I don't really like all this political stuff and she was sure I was just trying to bait her. But I showed her. I got all my friends together and we made up this great letter campaign, saying who I was and that I'd worked hard for the party and everything I'd done. I used my own allowance for stamps, and we ran them all off at Mom's office. We mailed them to all the voters, and then we phoned everyone we could think of to come out and vote.

Lara nominated me, much to Mom's dismay. And I won! I beat out one of the other youth delegates on the slate; not Lara but another one of Mom's assistants, Lucy. Mom felt so bad about it that she offered to pay for Lucy's observer status so she could still come and work. I couldn't believe I'd won. And now here I am. A delegate.

Green House is an old log cabin set back in the grounds, with a fenced-in courtyard outside. Inside there's a big fireplace, and booths set up all around the walls. I am directed to the Winnipeg South booth. It's not too crowded so it's easy to find. A young woman who looks familiar smiles at me.

"Ali?"

I nod.

"I thought I recognized you. Here's your kit. Go over to that table for your hat and T-shirt."

I try not to squint at her name tag so she doesn't notice that I don't remember her name. Everyone remembers me but it's awfully hard for me to remember all these faces. Oh yeah, Mabel Lukowitch, she was head of volunteers for Mom's campaign. I smile and follow her directions. At the table a kid my brother's age smiles at me and says "Hi." I

16

see from his tag he's from B.C. All tags say where you're from as well as your name.

"Oh." He grins, looking at my name. "Guess you'll be working hard over the next few days."

"Guess so," I say.

"My name is Rob," he says and he hands me a hat and a red T-shirt with Green written across it in green letters against a big white Maple Leaf.

I look at it and make a face.

"Well," Rob says, "it's not *haute couture*, but it's nice and bright. We'll let you know when our first meeting is," he says. "We'll meet each morning to let the delegates know what's going on during the day. After that you'll get together separately with the youth leader from your constituency. There's lots of work to do. We have to try to convince as many of the other delegates as we can to come over to us. *And* we have to make sure we don't lose any of our own."

Just then, someone else comes up behind me.

"Hi!" Rob says to the new arrival. To me, he calls, "See you tomorrow."

I take the hint and wander off. I realize that I *will* have to work really hard. Even though part of me doesn't even want Mom to win, and part of me doesn't even want to be here, I'd better pull up my socks. After all, those people elected me to come as a delegate for Rosaline Green and it's up to me to do my part.

I sure showed Mom, didn't I?

DAY 2

WEDNESDAY, JULY 6

7 A.M.

I don't like mornings. I like to stay up late and sleep all morning. That's my big plan for this summer because next year I'll have to get a job. This summer I can just hang out. Unless we have to move. That'll change everything.

Mom spent last night huddled in her suite going over and over questions for the forum this morning. The forums are a series of leadership debates sponsored by different groups in the party. There's a youth forum, a women's forum, and an aboriginal forum. In each one the questions will focus on the things which really concern those groups. Mom's two top advisors, Cathy Miller and Saul Leiper, would ask her questions and she'd answer. If she got it wrong, Cathy or Saul would correct her and then she'd do it all again. I listened for a while. It was mostly boring except when Mom got into a fight with Cathy about day care. Cathy said we can't afford universal day care and Mom said we'd just better find the money. Cathy said Mom was promising to spend too much money and the delegates wouldn't like it. Mom wouldn't budge. She's very stubborn. But I'm not sure she's right. After all, where is she going to find all this money? Cathy sounded pretty convincing. But then, so did Mom. She said she's going to tax big business for the money. And Cathy said if Mom did that, they'd stop giving money to the party and the party would never get elected. And Mom said, "Who runs this country anyway, government or big business?" And then Cathy and Saul looked at each other and laughed and said, "Big business." Mom didn't laugh. She just said, "Not for long," in this real serious voice. They stopped laughing. Then it got really boring so I decided to go swimming.

The pool was actually full of people but I didn't know any of them. I felt a bit shy. A few were my age but they didn't talk to me. I just did some laps, then went back to the room. I fell asleep after watching a bunch of reruns. Lara came in around 2 A.M. I think.

The wake-up call just about sent me through the roof. I had to answer it because Lara refused to. Now she's lying in bed moaning.

"It couldn't be morning already," she mutters, her face buried in the pillow.

"Yes, it is," I reply. "It's seven o'clock and *you* have a meeting at eight. Why does that mean *I* have to get woken up at seven?"

"You don't," she mutters. "Go back to sleep. We'll have breakfast at eight-thirty in your mom's room. Just tell me what you want and I'll order it up."

"I'll have orange juice and French toast."

Lara staggers out of bed and into the bathroom. I try to go back to sleep but the shower is too noisy and, of course, she has to have "Canada A.M." on while she's dressing.

Lara has great taste. She has long black hair and dark brown eyes and very fair skin—in fact most people think she's my older sister, which I take as a compliment 'cause she's very pretty—and she always wears the neatest clothes. I mean they aren't wild or anything but they're very with it. Today she's in a white suit with a real short skirt and flats. She's quite tall and hardly ever wears heels. Besides, she says she's on her feet too much and heels are the invention of some sadistic male, along with panty hose and bras. Mom tells her that she shouldn't complain because when Mom was a teenager, all the girls wore girdles, and bras with bones in them. Mom was skinny as a rail but still wore a girdle. Until university and hippies and flower power—then the women threw their bras and girdles away. Mom still hates wearing a bra, but hey—when you're a member of Parliament you can't run around bra-less, in love beads and tie-dyed T-shirts. No, she wears Ports and Alfred Sung now. Long way from the bell bottoms and head bands of university.

Anyway, after Lara leaves I switch the channel and watch some cartoons. I still like cartoons. So I'm fourteen and I like cartoons. Big deal. I flip back and forth occasionally to see if I can catch some stories about the convention.

This morning is the first leadership debate of the convention and it's sponsored by the youth delegates, so the candidates are supposed to address our concerns. Mom asked me what my concerns were. I told her they should find us somewhere better to hang out than 7 Eleven. She nodded and wrote that down. I think mostly it'll be about university funding, education, and stuff like that. I think kids should be given more responsibility for their own education. Like no one should *make* them go to school. They should go because they *want* to go. And if school was interesting enough, everyone would want to go, and no one would skip classes because they'd feel too guilty. I told Mom that. She said that's the way it would be in a perfect world.

I decide to shower and dress and check out the action in Mom's suite. I put on a pair of cut-offs and my Green T-shirt, which saves me fifteen minutes of trying to decide which shirt to wear. But my hair won't go right and all the cover-up in the world won't hide this huge zit I have. I feel like staying in the hotel room. Finally I make myself go next door so I won't have to eat a cold breakfast.

About ten people are sitting around the big table, drinking coffee and going over all the morning newspapers, especially the Calgary ones the delegates will be reading.

"It's hopeless," Cathy Miller sighs.

Everyone sort of waves at me when I come in, then they carry on as if I'm not there.

"These papers are so conservative, they'll try and squash all of us, but especially you, Ros. Jeez, I'm sorry James managed to swing the votes to get this thing in Calgary."

"It's his kind of city, that's for sure," Saul pipes in. "Business all the way. They'll come out for him in an editorial on Saturday before the vote. Just watch."

"It's not the editorial I mind," Mom says, running her fingers through her cropped black hair, obviously angry, "it's the bias of their reporting. They take a story that's supposed to be unslanted and slant it so far it's practically on its side."

I wander over to look at the headlines.

"Green Slides Fast!" the big letters scream. "James Takes Over." That's from the big daily.

The tabloid has a large picture of a snowflake and beside it a picture of Mom. "James Calls Green a Flake," the headline yells.

"He said it was flaky to promise to spend too much

24

money and the corporations *are* paying their fair share," she says. "Like hell they are."

"We'd better be careful," Saul says. "I smell something fishy. I think the fix is in, Ros, and there's a lot of big money out there that doesn't want you to win."

Mom nods glumly and picks up another paper. They continue to go over everything and discuss how they can get some better media coverage today.

"Don't respond directly to these accusations," Saul advises. "Be positive. Tell the youth all the things *you'll* do. And put James on the spot. Make him say what, if anything, he's going to do for the young. And don't forget, it's not the public that votes Saturday, it's *these* delegates. We have to target them and worry about the public later."

Finally, the meeting breaks up and almost everyone leaves. Breakfast arrives and Mom, Lara, Cathy, Saul, and I eat together. Then we all get ready to go.

"There'll be a crowd downstairs, Ali," Mom warns. "Be ready!"

We go down the elevator. On the main floor, Mom is mobbed by reporters the minute the elevator doors open.

"Ms. Green"—Mom insists on Ms., not Mrs.—"how do you respond to your opponent's criticism?"

"The delegates will decide who has the soundest policies and who has the interest of the ordinary Canadian at heart," Mom replies. She's always calm, never gets flustered. I don't have a terrible temper but I get upset way easier than she does. She says that's just age and I'll grow out of it.

Cathy and Saul answer some questions and Mom manages to dodge the reporters long enough to shake hands with some of the delegates in the lobby. Then we stagger through the mob until we're in a waiting car.

Whew! I don't like crowds, and sometimes crushes like

that can get scary. I look forward to arriving at the grounds and getting away from Mom and her entourage. Even being on my own, which is pretty nerve-racking, is better than this. She just loves the limelight. I find it *totally* embarrassing.

10 A.M

Lara and I squeeze through the mob of reporters that greet our car's arrival, and I follow her into the Roundup centre. It's a very different place today than yesterday, because today there are people everywhere. A huge corridor connects to the outer doors on one side and the huge meeting halls on the other. In the corridor each candidate has information booths set up. There are also booths selling buttons, hats, and paraphernalia for the candidates as well as booths with souvenirs of Calgary and the convention, a table full of beautiful native jewellery, and tables where Liberal ridings from across Canada exhibit T-shirts, rings, mugs, and posters. There are also lots of concession stands selling hot dogs, drinks, and snacks.

Lara is anxious to get to the Centre Hall where the forum will be, because she's one of the youth organizers, so I don't have time to stop at each booth, as I'd like to. One button does catch my eye and, as a cartoon fan, I can't resist it. I fork over a loony and am rewarded with a large button with a very angry Bullwinkle moose on it. Around the top, "Great Canadian Folklore #1 in a Series," is written. Beneath this are the words, "Contrary to popular belief Bullwinkle the Moose is not, and never has been, leader of the P.C. Party of Canada . . ." then in red print, "And he resents the connection." I giggle and pin it to my T-shirt. Then I follow Lara through the milling crowd. We pass the media room, which I peek into. It is set up with a few TV sets and lots of long tables. It has a sort of stage at the far end, and along the side are little sections for the print media. I am shoved away as I don't have media credentials, but I manage to catch a glimpse of my mother's least favourite TV announcer. She says he and his wife are often over at the prime minister's for cocktails and it shows in their reporting, which is completely biased towards the government.

"Here we go, Robert, here we go!
Here we go, Robert, here we go!"

We are suddenly overtaken by a mob of about twenty or thirty kids who are screaming their lungs out and marching down the corridor with their candidate Heraux in the centre. I actually like Heraux and so does Mom. He's really a funny guy with a great sense of humour. He has three small children, he lives in Ottawa and when our whole family was there once, he and his wife had us all over for dinner. We had the best food I've ever eaten—a kind of fancy stew that was actually delicious. Mom's stew is practically inedible, but she says she doesn't have to be a good cook as long as she's a good lawyer and a good M.P. Too bad for us. Dad's a good cook when he takes the time. French food is much better than Jewish food as far as I'm concerned. I mean outside of chicken soup you just can't compare. Italian is my real favourite though—I could eat pasta for breakfast, lunch, and dinner.

Anyway, Heraux's considered to be in third place, and if Mom wasn't running I'd vote for him. He's kinda short, with thick wavy black hair and a great smile. Actually he's pretty good looking for an older guy.

We follow the Heraux kids into the hall. This group just marches along the rear of the hall to the far door, yelling all the way, a few cameras in tow, and then Heraux disappears out the far door.

"Over there," Lara says, pointing.

It is a massive cavern of a room. Hanging from the iron beams that traverse the high ceiling are huge posters of all the candidates and big red and white Liberal signs. In the centre of the room is a very large, raised square platform built for TV cameras and their operators. The room is filled with long tables and chairs and already half-filled with people. And of course in the front of the room is a long table on a raised section where the candidates will sit.

I can see Lara is pointing to a sea of green hats just in front of the media stand, right in the centre of the room.

"Come on."

I follow her. She sits me in a chair at a table that directly faces the candidates' table. I recognize a few of the people around me; three are from our riding, others from other ridings in Winnipeg. I must be the youngest here. Most seem to be eighteen or older, although there are a few sixteen-year-olds. Though "youth" is anyone from fourteen to twenty-five, not too many fourteen-year-olds get to come. Soon Lara is bringing people from all over Manitoba to sit with us. She introduces me to another girl, Lauralee, who's a bit older than me and comes from Thompson.

I see a number of the organizers, Lara, Jonathan Sokol,

Richard Morris, scurrying around giving instructions to everyone. Jonathan, who is the youth leader for Winnipeg South, comes over to us and says, "Don't leave your seats. We have the perfect spot here and James's people are just waiting to grab these seats if we leave. Don't worry. We have other kids for the demo when Rosaline enters. You're important for the cameras. Every time they shoot that table with the candidates, they're going to catch a sea of Green hats in their shot."

He disappears, but in five minutes he's back. "Oh, and don't boo James. Instead, if *he* says anything to attack us, we yell a Green chant. Let's always be positive."

In the meantime the chairpersons are conducting the biennial meeting of the Young Liberals of Canada. I can't say I'm really interested in what's going on. Everyone on the floor is talking to each other and not paying too much attention either. I get to know the kids sitting around me. They tell me where they're from and how they got nominated and everything. Finally someone announces lunch. It's a boxed lunch and is given out at the back. Everyone has to take turns going to get it so we don't lose our seats. I go and get mine while this girl Terry from Winnipeg North holds my seat. I open my lunch to find a mini potato salad, a ham and cheese sandwich, and an orange. I'm not used to eating ham so I trade with Terry, who got a cheese and tomato sandwich.

The two chairpersons, a young woman and a young man, get up and begin to introduce the program. They speak for a while about Young Liberals and what it's all about and how the forum will run. They say they will ask the candidates questions that are already prepared. These questions will be drawn from a hat. I feel sorry for the young man. His French is pretty bad, and since he has to speak in both

English and French he must be a bit embarrassed.

I am sitting two seats from an aisle and suddenly, leaning over the table, his face in mine, is Alexander James's son, Paul. My heart lurches.

"Hi!" He grins.

Automatically my hand goes to cover my name tag but his eyes are faster. Then I think about my zit but it would be too obvious to try to cover that as well so I stop myself, but I'm ready to die of embarrassment.

"Alison Green. Green," he repeats. "Hmm. Familiar name. Any relation?"

"Mother," I answer, blushing.

"Well, I bet we'd have lots to talk about." He smiles.

He's completely relaxed, not at all shy and self-conscious like most of the boys I know.

"Maybe," I say.

"I'll catch up with you later," he says, making it almost sound like a date. "Okay?"

I shrug.

"Sure, I guess."

"See you."

"Yeah, see you."

He moves off to join the James group which is just off to our left. Lara is standing beside me and it's like everyone around me stopped doing everything, even breathing while we were talking. They are all staring at me. I am blushing so hard my whole body feels hot and I realize I have broken out in a sweat.

I have to say something, anything.

"Maybe he'll tell me all their secrets," I offer.

Lara laughs. The others don't join her but at least everyone stops staring at me and gets back to business. I try to slow my heart which is beating so fast I feel like it couldn't be healthy, and I try to calm down. Why would he do that? Could he like me? Or is he really after our secrets? Man, this is an unexpected turn of events!

There is a huge roar from the crowd to our right and Heraux enters the room again.

"Here we go, Robert,
here we go!" (clap, clap)
"Here we go, Robert
here we go!" (clap, clap)

A sea of red and white pours into the room as Heraux stops to shake hands and talk.

Moments later another group enters, all blue and white, very noisy, yelling "Potter, Potter, Potter!" He's the 'Right to Life' guy. Actually, I heard him speak at the leadership debate in Winnipeg and he's not as stupid as I thought he'd be but I don't think any person has the right to tell another person what to do. Like, there was this girl in one of the other grade nine classes this year. And she got pregnant. She had to drop out of school and she's a real mess. I mean, who's to say she shouldn't have had an abortion? That baby is going to have a hard life. And Mom gets really mad at Potter because he doesn't support programs like day care for the children who *are* alive. He thinks all mothers should stay home. Well, that's okay for some, but what if you *want* to work outside of your home? Or what if you *have* to?

"Let's go, James,
let's go!
Let's go, James,
let's go!"

A huge mob now comes in with James and they're coming down the aisle. The whole hall is in pandemonium. TV cameras, flash bulbs, reporters, everyone is chasing James. Two minutes later Mom's group comes in; and what

I thought of as a huge mob around James seems small compared to hers.

"Way to go, Green,
way to go!
Way to go, Green,
way to go!"

Lara is here.

"Up on the chairs!" she orders everyone. We all leap up and wave our placards and yell at the top of our lungs.

"Hey hey, hey ho,
Green is the way to go!
Hey hey, hey ho,
Green is the way to go!
Green! Green! Green! Green!"

Every time we scream her name, we push our placards up into the air.

The candidates make their way to the podium. They take their seats. The chairpersons introduce them. One by one the crowd cheers their own. The noise level is unbelievable.

I look over to the James camp. Paul is on the table waving a placard. He glances over at me. Oh no! He caught me looking at him. I look away, really embarrassed. What a stupid thing to do. He's so tall, he's head and shoulders over most of the kids there and pretty easy to spot. Boy, he's cute.

The candidates start to answer questions about university funding and stuff like that.

Alexander James says that if Mom keeps all her promises, the country will have no money for *any* programs, and that she's being irresponsible.

She shoots back.

"Alex," she says, "I'd like to see you *make* some promises to these young people here. Promise them an end to child poverty, a good education, a chance in the world. Promise to give them somewhere else to go but the local 7 Eleven." All right, Mom! "Oh, and one more thing. I've always thought of the snowflake as one of the most beautiful things in the world. Each one is different and yet, together, they create something we call winter. I'd like to think of that as a symbol of Canada, lots of individuals coming together to create a country. I may just stick a little snowflake on every one of my posters to remind the candidates what this fight is all about."

The Green crowd goes wild. Good one, Mom! All her supporters are on their feet, screaming and yelling, and we don't stop for a good few minutes. What a come-back. She's good, my mom. Good and tough. I can vouch for that personally. Like when she says no she means no and that is that. Can't change her mind, even by throwing a tantrum. It's depressing.

I feel like looking over at Paul again but I stop myself. Take that, I think. I wonder if he agrees with his dad or if he really pays attention to what his dad is saying at all. I find a lot of it hard to follow and some of it really boring. But it *is* his dad and he's obviously behind him. I can feel the butterflies in my stomach. I wonder what "catch you later" means, *exactly*.

2 P.M.

After the debate, I wander down the corridors of the Roundup Centre. I'm to meet Lara at 5 P.M. but for now I'm on my own.

It's strange to be surrounded by kids who feel so passionate about Mom getting elected that they'd do almost anything to make it happen. It makes me feel sort of out of it by comparison. Still, I must admit that while the debate was on, I forgot all about the move and could only think about doing my best to put on a good show and help her get elected. I'm not usually too outgoing, I guess. I mean I'm not *shy*—well, not with kids or anything. But I'd rather die than get up in front of people and make a speech or even just stand on the stage with Mom. Maybe that's why Mike and I have taken to politics so differently. He is like Mom, just loves the limelight.

Suddenly a tall young man is blocking my way. I try to

get around him, but he moves as I move. He's unrolling something. He holds it in front of my face. It's so close to me that at first I can't make out what it is. Then I realize— it's a poster of a baby. I look at the guy's buttons—sure enough, "Potter for Life" in blue and white, stuck to his shirt and his hat.

"Know what this is?" he asks.

"Of course," I say, trying to get past.

"It's a baby. Your candidate wants to kill them. Do you really think that's right?"

"Do you think it's right for you to be able to order people around and make them do things?" I answer back, stung into an angry reply. I try to remember what Mom has said. "Why don't you try to worry about children who are alive and need help?"

He sticks the poster closer to my face.

"Murder. That's what it is. You want to support a candidate that supports murder?"

"You want to see murder?" a familiar voice crackles behind me. "Just keep shoving that thing in my friend's face."

I whirl around to see Paul standing there, hands on hips, glaring at this Potter delegate.

"Get lost, you jerk."

The jerk smiles at Paul. "No need to get upset."

The jerk moves away.

"Rescued!" says Paul, with a self-satisfied grin.

"I didn't need rescuing, thanks very much," I retort as I continue to walk. "Haven't you heard, knights in white armour aren't in any more. I was doing just fine."

I sneak a glance at him and see that he's blushing. Got him.

"Yeah, right, sorry."

He continues to walk along beside me.

"Where're you going?" he asks finally.

36

"Dunno. Just hanging around for a bit. Then I have to go over to Green House and meet a group of kids. We're going to go 'round and talk to delegates."

"Want to grab a burger or something up at the cafeteria?"

I'm actually starving. That little lunch was not enough to keep anyone alive. But should I be seen with James's son? Should I even be talking to him?

"Sure," I say. "I'm hungry."

"Me too," he agrees. "That lunch wasn't enough to feed a four-year-old."

He seems to know his way around, so I follow his lead up to the second-floor cafeteria. We each get a burger, fries, and Coke. It's not as crowded as I'd expected, but I guess most people aren't taking the time to eat if they're on the grounds.

We sit down. Suddenly I'm so tongue-tied I feel like I could die. Why did I say yes?

"So," he says, "what grade are you in?"

He's asking me a normal question. I almost faint with relief. I was sure he'd start talking politics.

"Going into ten. What about you?"

"Same."

"Have you always lived in Montreal?" I ask. Of course he knows where I'm from and I know where he's from, so we can't ask each other that.

"Yeah."

"You speak perfect English," I say. "I mean—" (oh I'm so stupid) "not the least bit of an accent or anything."

"Dad spoke English to me and Mom spoke French and I went to French school." He grins. "You always lived in Winnipeg?"

"Yeah."

"Like it?"

"It's okay. Probably not as exciting as Montreal."

"Probably not," he agrees.

37

"Well," I reply, feeling I have to defend it now, "it's a lot cleaner though! Not so polluted. I hate the air down east. It stinks."

"True. But we have cafés to go to and hang out at, and blues bars and stuff. I hear you guys hang out at 7 Eleven."

I laugh.

"Right." Got me there. I pause. I can't resist asking, "Think your dad will win?"

"Yeah, I do," he answers. "He's got Quebec. Your mom can't win without it."

"She has lots of delegates from Quebec," I protest.

"Yeah, she got them before Dad entered. But he got most after that and I've heard that more are jumping ship and coming over to us."

"Really?" I say. I'd better ask Lara if it's true.

"Do you like all this?" I ask.

He knows right away what I mean.

"Well, I'm probably more used to it than you are. After all, Dad's been an M.P. for eleven years now and I'm just, well, almost fifteen. I hardly remember anything else." He looks up. "Don't see him at all really," he says, and he sounds angry even though I can see he's trying to stay cool.

I nod. "Yeah, I know what you mean. Except my mom manages to breathe down my neck even when she's not around. When's your birthday?" I don't know why I ask that, just something about the way he'd said he's almost fifteen.

"July 7."

"Tomorrow?"

"Yeah."

"What are you doing for it?"

"It won't be the first time there's no time for a birthday party." He grins. But I can see he really doesn't think that's too funny. "When's yours?"

38

"Mine? December 15."

"I'm *much* older than you," he says, in a serious voice.

"Everyone's much older than me," I groan. "I'm always the youngest in my class."

I realize I haven't even touched my fries and he hasn't even had a bite out of his burger.

"We'd better eat," I say. "I have to be at a meeting soon."

"Oh? What meeting?"

"I'm not telling," I reply.

"What are you doing tonight after the Women's Forum?"

I try not to choke on the gulp of Coke I just took. This sounds awfully like a date invitation. I haven't dated a lot, although in grade seven I "went out" with about ten different boys. That meant I hung out with one of them at school until we broke up and I'd hang out with someone else. By grade eight I thought that was babyish. In grade nine, a group of us did everything together—my girlfriends and sometimes a few guys we get along with. I must say, I like Paul. But he's James's son. I mean, Mom would have a fit. As soon as I think about Mom, something inside takes over and I hear myself saying, "Nothing. Probably just watching another movie on pay TV."

"Want to do something?"

"Like?"

"I don't know. Catch a late movie at one of the theatres near our hotels."

For a moment I pause.

"Look," he says, "I'll meet you in front of the media room after the forum. You can tell me then."

"Okay," I say, pushing back my chair. "I gotta run now. See you later."

I practically sprint out of the restaurant, down the stairs, and outside. I don't slow down until I'm on the paved walkway that leads to Green House. My heart is pounding, my hands are damp with sweat. Man, what a mess! I'm falling for the son of Mom's biggest enemy. She doesn't like James. I know that. She thinks he's sneaky and ruthless and all wrong in his beliefs. Yipes. How do I ask her if I can go out with his son? And yet I know that shocking her into paying some attention to me outside of "Have you done your homework?" or "When will you be home?" is part of what made me want to say yes. Maybe she'll think he's just trying to get information out of me or something. I stop while I'm walking. Is that possible? Could he be using me to get to know stuff about Mom? I've got to talk to Lara about this. She'll know what to do.

I hope so. Because I sure don't.

5 P.M.

I am in my hotel room waiting to speak to Lara. Mom has been in her suite most of the afternoon working like crazy on her big speech for Friday night. She's also being briefed for the debate tonight sponsored by the Women's Commission. Every once in a while a group of delegates are brought in to meet her.

I spent the rest of this afternoon campaigning. First we had a meeting at Green House. We sat outside on the grass, ten of us and our group leader, Jonathan. He asked us how things were going and if we were clear about what we were supposed to do. Then he showed us how to go about approaching delegates. He said that if we spot anyone who isn't wearing a button, we should go up and offer them a Green button. If they say no, we ask why and get them talking. We talk about her policies and how great she'll be and see if they want to meet her. If they do, we try to arrange that by contacting

Jonathan or someone else at Green House. Everyone is quite a lot older than me and I felt funny about doing that by myself, so I latched onto Terry. She's really nice. She's about eighteen, and she has boundless energy without coming across as pushy. She would go up to people and talk to them, no problem. By around four o'clock I was pretty tired though, and I decided to take a cab back to the hotel. Mom has suddenly forgotten to be overprotective. She's just too busy now.

I found it hard to concentrate on anything all afternoon after that lunch with Paul. I don't really know why I like him so much, I just do. Well, he *is* really good looking, and really nice, and sympathetic and he seems pretty smart, too. And he's not geeky like most of the boys I know. I mean he doesn't have to show off to make an impression. I like that. He's got lots of confidence, too—something I wish I had a bit more of.

We'd all arranged to meet here for an early supper at five. The forum tonight starts at seven. Finally I hear Lara's key in the door. She comes in and collapses on the bed.

"Hi, Ali. How'd it go today?"

"Good. How 'bout you?"

"Crazy. But good."

"Good."

"I want to have a quick shower," Lara continues, "and change." She drags herself off the bed. "Did you know that Terry and a huge group of kids are staying just a couple of floors down?"

"No," I reply, "I didn't."

"You should go down and see them tonight," Lara suggests. "They're lots of fun. I'm sure they'd be glad to include you."

"Ah . . . about tonight," I start, my heart pounding.

Lara is already in the bathroom, the shower going.

"What?" she yells.

42

"Nothing," I yell back. "I'll tell you when you get out."

If I yell it to her, the entire hotel will hear.

Five minutes later she emerges from the shower, towel wrapped around her.

I start again. "Well, guess who I bumped into after the forum?"

She's getting dressed, but it must be something in my voice that makes her look up. She pulls on a bright red dress, then steps into red flats.

"Not . . . *Paul?*" she grins.

"How'd you know?" I ask, feeling slightly offended that she guessed so easily.

"The way he was eyeing you," she replies. "Like a spider after a fly."

I grab my brush and try to do something with my hair so I can keep from showing how uncomfortable this is making me. I want to sound really casual.

"Yeah, well, we went and grabbed a bite and he's actually okay."

"Oh?"

"Yeah, and," I rush on, "he wants to catch a movie or something tonight."

To my absolute shock, Lara answers with a resounding "*No.*"

"What?" I say, not really believing this is Lara talking.

"No, Ali, and I don't even want you to ask your mom. Look, we don't really know him, we don't know what he's after. Maybe he's using you to get information or he's trying to convert you—*that* would be a coup for his side. Or maybe he can't be trusted and you'll get into an awkward situation and won't know how to get out of it without creating some sort of major scene that'll be gobbled up by the million news hounds who are bound to find out."

I stare at Lara. I thought she was my friend. Now she sounds like nothing more than a political advisor.

"But I like him," I find myself saying.

She takes a deep breath. "Okay Ali. You like him. And if we win you'll see *lots* of him in Ottawa. He's often there visiting his dad and I've even heard they're going to move if his dad wins in the next election."

"Or if he wins *this*," I interrupt. "That's possible too."

"Yes, it is," she says. "It is possible. It's looking *very* close in fact. And we can't have you doing anything that could mess up your mom's chances. People will say if she can't control a fourteen-year-old, *then* what? People expect you to behave."

"It's just a movie!" I protest.

"Look, I'm not saying not to see him. Although I'd be careful. Very careful. If he's anything like his dad, I wouldn't trust him for a second. Still, tomorrow morning is the pancake breakfast. You can see him there. There's a dance tomorrow night after the tribute to Croix. You can see him there. Just don't start with this dating business."

The phone rings. Lara picks it up.

"Yes, I'll be right there." She hangs up.

"Come on. We should go next door. Time for supper."

As usual, we're ordering up. It's too difficult to eat around mobs of people.

"Come on, Ali. Don't look at me that way. Just think about what's on the line here. It's the future of the country. How does that compare to a movie date?"

"Well," I mutter defiantly, "I don't think a movie date will affect the 'future of the country.' I really don't."

I'm starting to get mad.

"No, I'm sure you're right," Lara smiles. "I'm probably being completely unreasonable. But how about indulging me on this one. *Please*?"

I stare at her. Should I just ask Mom? *She* might say yes. But Lara thinks it could somehow turn out bad for Mom. And the truth is I'm pretty nervous about it myself. Still, if I get a chance, I will ask Mom. I can't believe it. After all the time Lara and I have spent together, all she can think of is how this'll look. What about me? What about my happiness? Doesn't that count at all?

9 P.M.

I'm in a section over to the right of the hall and I have a placard that I'm pushing up and down with the other youth delegates around me, all of us shouting "Green, Green, Green." My arm is practically breaking. The forum is over and the candidates are filing off the stage. Mom did really well. I thought the men looked and sounded stiff in comparison to her and they just weren't as comfortable talking about women's issues. Heraux was actually the best next to her. Baker was just awful. He kept saying women want this, women want that, as if he knew, and Potter kept going on and on about abortion. James sounded phoney to me but he had a lot of support.

I give my placard to Jonathan and push my way through the crowd. I'm going to the media room. I never had a chance to ask Mom and I didn't want to get into a big fight with her so I've just decided to go to the movies. I'm old enough to go to a stupid movie no matter what Lara says. Maybe Paul is a jerk like his dad, but then again maybe he isn't. The only way to find out is to spend some time with him. I hurry down the corridor, keeping my eyes open for Paul and for Lara. I don't want her to stop me. He's not in front of the media room when I get there. I search the crowds milling around but he's nowhere to be seen. If he doesn't hurry, Lara will find me. I pace around impatiently, my stomach a mass of butterflies.

Finally I see him. He bursts through a group of kids, in his red and white James T-shirt and cut-offs. Just my outfit, except of course I have on my Green T-shirt.

"Hi," he says, but he's not smiling. He looks upset. "Look, about tonight . . ."

He seems to lose his nerve and can't get the words out.

I guess he's changed his mind. It was a stupid idea anyway, going out with him. And I can suddenly see Terry, Lara, and all the kids from the Winnipeg delegation heading right for us. I decide to save myself any further humiliation.

"Listen, sorry. I just can't. I'm going with the Winnipeg group back to the hotel. See ya, okay?"

"Yeah, sure," he says, and I must say he looks really miserable.

As I start to leave, he calls after me.

"Gonna be at the pancake breakfast?"

"Guess so," I call back.

"Well, see you then."

I don't reply, unwilling to agree to meet him anywhere, any time, anyhow.

Terry grabs my arm.

"Come on, Ali. We're going back to the hotel to watch the news and see how it looks. Lara said you could come with us."

"Sure, great," I agree, trying to put on a brave face considering how disappointed and upset I feel.

"Ali," Lara says, "I'll go back to the hotel with your mom. We're meeting delegates here for a while. See you back there later."

"Okay," I say, allowing myself to be hustled into a cab by Terry and five other kids. The rest grab another cab and we're on our way. I quickly discover, however, that we're *not* going to the hotel.

"There's a social tonight, Ali. At Trappers Bar. And we thought you might as well come!"

"But I can't get into a bar," I exclaim. "I barely look fifteen, never mind eighteen."

"It's okay," Terry says. "There'll be such a crunch, they'll never notice you. Just don't order any booze and I'll bet no one'll bother you."

I almost ask to be taken back to the hotel, but then I remember Lara ordering me to behave and I suddenly don't want to behave. I want to live a little dangerously.

"Great," I say. "Sounds like fun."

We arrive at an old building right downtown. Everyone spills out of the cab after we all chip in for the fare. We go in the front door into a huge room on the ground floor. It is packed with people. Most seats are taken, and everyone is standing and talking. Terry grabs my hand and we move over to one side where we take a table with a couple of empty seats. Terry plunks me in one of them and herself in another. Others sit on the table edge or stand. Soon beer is brought but the waiter just ignores me. Guess he figures it's not worth the fight—he must see I'm under age.

All anyone can talk about is the convention, how Mom is doing, stuff like that. The room seems to surge and more people squeeze in. I can see lots of red and white shirts. I'm sure Paul won't be here, but plenty of James kids are.

I turn when voices just behind us are raised. A fight has started.

"You're throwing your vote away," a James kid yells. He looks around twenty years old. He also looks pretty drunk. "The Liberals can't win an election without Quebec and the only one who can take Quebec is James. You vote for Green and she wins, we'll lose the next election. Do you want that? You want five more years of Tory government? Then we won't *have* a country left."

"Yeah?" replies the Green kid he's fighting with, who also looks like he's had one too many. "Well, voting for James is just like voting Tory. He's all big business and he's secretly for free trade even though he won't admit it."

"He may have a good business sense but that doesn't mean he'll cut on social programs."

"Yes, it does! Don't let him fool you!"

"No, you're the fool." This is accompanied by a push.

"Hey, man, back off."

"No, you back off." Another push.

A bunch of kids from our group leap up at this point and separate them. Terry winks at me.

"Fun, eh?"

"Sure," I reply. "Lots of fun."

Actually I'm having an awful time. I can't breathe from the heat and the smoke, and I keep thinking how nice it would've been to go to a movie with Paul. What happened, I wonder? Did he decide he didn't like me? Did he meet someone else? Did he look so unhappy 'cause he was embarrassed to break off the date or was there another reason? Should I avoid him at the breakfast tomorrow or give him a chance to explain? Or maybe he'll avoid me 'cause he was trying to tell me it was all a mistake.

Terry pulls on my arm.

"How are you doing?" she yells over the din.

"Okay."

"Listen, I'm going back to the hotel soon. Wanna come?"

"Yes," I scream, jumping at the chance. "I do."

In ten minutes Terry and I leave. Once at the hotel she asks me if I want to catch the eleven o'clock news with her.

"Sure," I say.

Her room is an unbelievable disaster. There are clothes, towels, pillows, covers everywhere so you can hardly find a place to sit.

"Who's staying here?" I ask.

"Me, Linda, Kelly, May, Stuart, and Kyle."

"What?"

"Yeah, two in each bed, two on the floor."

She giggles. "In the morning we sneak down the corridor to steal towels from the maid's cart. After all," she says, replying to my shocked look, "none of us can really afford to be here in the first place. So we all share rooms, hardly eat, and almost never sleep."

And just so Mom can win. Makes me feel pretty stupid and petty when all I can think about is Mom's main opponent's son. Well, no more. As of tomorrow, I'll really go to work. Tomorrow is the official opening of the convention. Everyone will get down to business and so will I!

DAY 3

THURSDAY, JULY 7

7:30 A.M.

My T-shirt smells. I decide not to wear it today. Lara is up and in the shower. I'm laying out my clothes as I watch "Canada A.M." The coverage of Mom looks worse and worse—there's more and more negative talk about how her programs will be too expensive. They interview a James delegate who calls Mom a big spender with her head in the clouds. He says we need a good economy or we won't be able to afford anything. They barely mention how great she did in the debate last night. This is something I'm learning about the media. They can really slant a story the way they want. By *not* talking about all the issues she dealt with yesterday and focusing on all the negative stuff, they make her sound practically stupid. She had some great shots at all the men last night but you'd never know it.

When Lara gets out of the shower, I take my turn. I rinse my T-shirt out and hang it up to dry. Maybe I can change back into it later today. Or maybe Lara can use her pull to get me a second one. After all, what's the use of being the candidate's daughter if you don't have any perks?

I put on a clean pair of cut-offs and then try on all my T-shirts to see which one I should wear. My zit burst last night, but now it's all scaly and red. I plaster cover-up over it. Finally I decide on my Save the Earth T-shirt.

"Lara, how about getting me an extra T-shirt?"

She looks at me and pretends to be horrified.

"Why, Ali, that wouldn't be fair! We have to set a good example. We can't get better treatment than the other delegates. You should walk around smelling like everyone else."

"Thanks a lot, Lara," I grimace.

"And thank you for listening to me about last night," she says. "You did the right thing."

"Whatever," I reply, not mentioning that it was Paul who stood *me* up.

Just before eight o'clock, we go next door to Mom's suite for breakfast. Like yesterday, the papers are spread out on the table and everyone is going over them while drinking their coffee. By the looks on their faces, I can tell the news isn't good.

"Green Spends More Money!" yells the Calgary daily.

"Heraux and James Challenge Green!" reads the Calgary tabloid.

"Why don't they just report what happened last night?" I ask.

"Because these newspapers are all owned by conservatives and your Mom is much too far away from conservative thinking," Cathy answers. "James is their man and they'll slant everything to suit that—not just the editorials but the so-called 'objective' stories, too."

She gets up from the table and starts to pace.

"If we can't get good coverage for a debate you obviously won," she says to Mom, "I don't know what they'll do to you if you just do the same as the rest."

"They'll slaughter me," Mom says. "They'll say I'm weak and I can't cut it. And don't tell me," she says to no one in particular, "that part of this coverage isn't because I'm a woman. I have to be twice as smart as they are just to pull up equal. Makes me sick."

"I'm starting to hear anti-Jewish stuff," Saul Leiper says, his voice low.

"What?" Mom exclaims.

"Yeah, a number of Green delegates have been approached by James people. 'Do you know Green is Jewish?' they ask. One said, 'No' and looked surprised. 'Oh yes,' was the reply. 'She's Jewish. And so's everyone running her campaign!' "

Mom sinks down on the sofa.

"Well, I shouldn't be surprised. When it looked like I might win the last election, those things started to surface too. A Jew and a woman. Double whammy."

She pauses. "Look. We have to go on the offence. We have to show that James doesn't have any credentials except that he's rich. We have to show him up to be the conservative he really is. And let's not forget Heraux. He's creeping up on us, isn't he? Has anyone talked to him about a second-ballot move?"

"I've talked to his people," Saul says. "I think they're with us, but I don't know what James is offering him. Some kind of deal, I'm sure."

They're talking about the final vote. If someone wins on the first ballot, it's all over then and there. But if there's no clear winner, then everyone votes again, on the second ballot. Usually the candidates that have the lowest numbers will drop off for the second ballot, like maybe Baker and *hopefully* Potter, and then there are more votes for the candidates that are left. It can even go to a third ballot or a fourth when the top two run against each other. And each time a candidate drops out of the race, he or she can throw their support *and* their delegates to one of the other candidates.

Mom wants to make sure that Heraux throws his support her way if he drops out. They talk about these possible scenarios over and over again so that they're prepared no matter what happens. Unfortunately Potter will probably go for James or even Heraux, and Baker might well go for James, too. Heraux could be what they call the "king maker." If he's in third place, whoever he throws his support to will probably win. Of course it could be Mom who's second or third and then she'll have to decide who to support. She'd go to Heraux, never James. But what if *both* she and Heraux are really close behind James—who will give up first?

Mom has juice and toast and coffee in the room already. Cold toast is such a treat. But there's a pancake breakfast, so we have to get ready to go to that. I still haven't decided whether to ignore Paul or not.

I figure I probably won't see him anyway. There will be so many people there that the chances of continuing to bump into him are really slim.

I sit down in a chair in the corner of the room and close my eyes. I'm tired. And there are three days left. I'm not really paying attention so I only catch the tail end of what Saul is saying.

"I heard about it weeks ago in Ottawa. If it's true, James is even more crooked than we'd thought."

"What?" I say, sitting up. "Crooked? James? How?"

Suddenly everyone is looking at me. I guess they'd forgotten I was here.

"Nothing, dear. Let's go!" says my mom. "I have to eat lots of pancakes for the cameras and shake lots of hands. How I can shake hands and eat I'm not sure, but let's give it a try."

"I'll stick by your side," Lara offers. "Just give me your plate whenever you need to."

"You've got it." Mom smiles.

We head down to the lobby. The elevator stops at almost every floor and fills up almost immediately. Everyone wants to shake Mom's hand and congratulate her on last night. "Keep it up!" they say. The lobby is even worse than yesterday. I guess all the reporters in Canada are in Calgary, and it's practically impossible to get to the waiting car. The lights from the cameras and the flashes are almost blinding. By the time we cram into the car, I have black spots in front of my eyes.

Mom is talking fast with Cathy and Saul, going over her schedule. Before tonight's tribute to the leader, Croix, we have a reception for delegates back at the hotel. She wants more time this afternoon to work on her speech. And then she has to sit through the tribute to Croix, whom she can't stand. He's not supporting her. In fact, he's working very hard behind the scenes for James.

I arrange to meet them all back at the hotel at five o'clock for the reception, which will be a barbecue dinner in the hotel courtyard.

We all get off at the site and Mom, as usual, is immediately surrounded by a planned demonstration of youth delegates. I slip away and head for the grassy grounds on the west side of the Roundup Centre, where the breakfast is being held. It's crowded but not unbearably so. There are long tables filled with flapjacks, eggs, and cartons of Beep. At the south end of the grassy lawn is a stage where a lively country and western band is performing. Haystacks are strewn throughout and people are sitting on them while they eat. I see James immediately. He is surrounded by reporters. He is talking fast and gesturing, no doubt telling more lies about Mom. I'm starting to really hate the guy. Has he told his people to use the fact that she's Jewish against her? I wonder. All that stuff about her being a flake and unstable—that's certainly coming from him.

He moves off to shake hands and Mom's entourage arrives. There must be sixty kids, all with placards, yelling "Green, Green" as she moves into the grounds. As soon as the media get some good shots of that they disperse a bit, so she can walk to the tables and they can get some shots of her eating. She does that. She's smiling and chatting with people around her. I wouldn't say she has the greatest sense of humour in the world, so she's probably *not* cracking jokes—which is too bad. I mean, she has a good sense of humour in that she likes to laugh and she loves Dad's jokes. She's just not too good at making jokes herself. Speech writers have to write her jokes for her and even then they come out sounding stiff.

Actually, James is not what I'd call a really funny guy, either. Heraux, on the other hand, is a riot—he's so quick, too. Say anything to him and he has a come-back in seconds. Wish I could do that.

I decide to eat my breakfast, then go to Green House to find out what I'm supposed to do today. I love pancakes, and I gobble down three of them soaked in syrup. They're cold but good. The drink is also very sweet and I start to feel a sugar rush. I can't help but keep one eye out for Paul, but I don't see him anywhere. Despite trying not to, I feel terribly disappointed.

The country band leaves, and we have some boring greetings from all kinds of dignitaries. Then an aboriginal group comes on stage. Their costumes are magnificent, bright yellow and silver or bright orange and silver. They do a couple of dances and then they announce a friendship circle. Paul still hasn't shown up. Is he trying to avoid me, or is the crowd just too big for us to find each other?

Terry finds me, though, and grabs me by the hand, dragging me into the friendship dance. Everyone holds hands and dances in a snake through the grounds. It's lots of fun.

"Can I cut in?"

Paul has come up behind us and asks the person on my left (Terry is on my right) if he can join. Of course they include him and suddenly he is holding my hand. His hand is twice the size of mine, smooth and warm. A tingle shoots from our hands straight through me.

"Hi," he says.

"Hi," I answer, trying to keep very cool, not even looking at him, reminding myself how much I'm coming to hate his dad.

"Can we talk later?"

"Why?" I ask.

"Please," he says, his voice urgent. "I just want to explain about last night. Oh, never mind later. How about now?"

He's actually pulling me out of the circle.

"Hey," I object, "I'm dancing!"

"Please!"

I drop Terry's hand, and Paul and I back away from the dancers. He looks around furtively, as if he's an escaped convict just waiting to be caught.

"I really wanted to go last night and I didn't know whether to tell you why I couldn't," he blurts out, "because I thought you'd think I have a really stupid family, but I decided last night that you'd be right if you thought that, so I want to tell you."

Then he stops and looks like he has no intention what-soever of actually telling me.

"Yes?" I say.

"Well, my dad wouldn't let me. Said I might say some-thing or give away a secret or get into trouble." He pauses again. "I think they think you can get a girl pregnant in a movie or something," he adds bitterly. "Or that *I* can."

I have to laugh. He grins back sheepishly.

"You aren't mad?"

"No, I wasn't allowed either. I was just going to go anyway."

Then he really looks like he'd like to crawl under the nearest haystack.

"Sorry," he says. "I guess I don't have enough guts."

"No, it's probably better we didn't go," I reply. "We don't want to cause a major incident or anything."

"You know my hotel is just around the corner from yours?" he says.

"Yeah." Where's this going?

"Well, how 'bout coming over for a swim sometime?"

I laugh. "Come on," I say, "can you imagine? Everyone there is a James delegate. They'll recognize me. I'll be lucky if I don't get drowned."

He has a definite twinkle in his eye—the look Mike gets when he's about to do something really bad.

"You think they'll get upset? Well, I do too."

"Hey," I answer, getting really ticked off. "Don't use me to get back at your dad. No way. Sorry."

He practically hangs his head.

"You're right. It's just—well, I never see him. I mean he eats at home maybe once a week, never asks me about anything, doesn't give a shit about me and now, suddenly he's watching my every move. But only because he's afraid I'll do something stupid to ruin his chances."

He pauses and starts to blush. "Sorry, you didn't want to hear all that."

"Yes, I do," I assure him, really impressed and a little embarrassed that he's telling me all this. "He's the exact opposite of my mom, actually. She's always hovering over me, driving me crazy, until the last couple of days 'cause she just doesn't have time any more. I like it *much* better this way."

"You wouldn't like it if she did that all the time," Paul says.

"No," I agree, "guess I wouldn't." And I realize that it's true, I wouldn't.

"Anyway," he says, obviously wanting to change the subject, "how 'bout tonight. Going to the rodeo?"

"Yes, but I'll be sitting with Lara."

"Not at the dance afterwards," he says, looking at his feet.

"No," I agree. "I guess not." I try to appear really cool and casual.

"I'll see you there, okay?"

"Sure, okay," I reply.

"I gotta go."

"Me too."

He takes off for a crowd of James supporters moving towards the James trailers. James has two big trailers he's using as a campaign headquarters. Only he and my mom are indoors. Heraux is in a huge tent and the other two really have nothing. Fortunately the weather is beautiful so it's not too bad for Heraux's gang.

The breakfast is breaking up and the official opening ceremonies will start in about fifteen minutes. I realize I'd better hustle over to Green House to check in with my group. I try to calm down—every time I see Paul my whole system seems to go haywire.

I wouldn't mind a dance with him tonight. Still, we'll probably never find each other. With almost seven thousand people here, it's a miracle he's been able to find me so often. Lara would probably tell me he's having me followed so he can gain my trust and then find out all our secrets. But I believed him when he said his father had said he couldn't see me. And I can't get over the way he confided in me like that. Man. I smile to myself. There's something about the idea of not being the "good" children, the "model" children, that really appeals to me. Could I have found an ally, here in the strangest place?

And then I have a terrible thought. It's his birthday and I forgot to wish him a Happy Birthday! Oh, how *could* I be so stupid and thoughtless. I'll have to find him tonight if only to give him birthday wishes. I may be the only one who remembers—I'll bet his dad won't. Suddenly tonight seems too far away.

8:15 P.M.

What a day! I try to sink back into my seat but of course the seat is too hard to do that with any comfort. The rodeo is about to begin. Lara and Terry are chatting together, and Mom is sitting just behind us with a group of her closest friends and advisors. It's been a really hectic day and yet parts of it were excruciatingly boring. First I went to our Winnipeg South youth meeting at Green House. Jonathan told us that we should spend the afternoon talking to delegates trying to convert them. The vote is now only two days away and every single delegate is important. We could win or lose on just a few votes. The leadership race is not the only business being taken care of at this convention. There's also all sorts of Liberal Party stuff like electing a new president of the party. That and motions and reports were scheduled all day so Jonathan advised us not to sit through it all but to wander the halls and go after delegates.

We went from the meeting at Green House to the opening ceremonies. Of course I felt like I'd already been here for weeks so it was weird to have "Official Opening Ceremonies" to sit through. There was some unexpected fun at the beginning of the session though. I sat there with Terry, preparing to be bored to death, when suddenly all the lights went out! I couldn't believe it. Well, within seconds the Heraux kids were on their feet screaming their heads off, "Way to go, Robert, way to go." They love him, they really do. It's a smaller group than ours but they *never* stop working. So we all jumped up and started yelling,

"Here we go, Ros, here we go!

Here we go, Ros, here we go!"

The James kids were up then screaming,

"Alex! Alex! Alex! Alex!"

Soon the entire room was one big demonstration. I guess that went on for at least ten minutes before they got the generator lights on. After that things got really boring, with opening ceremonies, rules of procedure, motions, and reports. I wandered around with Terry for a lot of it, talking to people. I met a delegate from Toronto named Maria, and we actually hit it off great and ended up talking through most of the morning. She's sixteen and has been working really hard for Mom. She's staying at the University of Calgary in a dorm 'cause it's cheap. Makes me realize what luxury I'm living in. Still, it sounds like she's having way more fun!

I grabbed a hot dog from one of the booths and then Maria and I spent the afternoon trying to talk to delegates. I know Mom is back at the hotel working on her speech. I was really upset when I bumped into the youth delegation from Portage Interlake at around 2 P.M. in the corridor. They had *all* switched to James and were wearing his T-

66

shirts and hats. I couldn't believe my eyes. When I asked them why, they said that he'd met them and talked to them and given them free pizza for lunch, and that Mom's people had been taking them for granted. Free pizza. Man, that was a serious political decision. I went over to Green House and left a message for Jonathan—it's the kind of thing he should know. I kept thinking about what he'd said about our winning or losing by just a few votes!

At 4:30 I grabbed a cab back to the hotel and quickly changed into a skirt and sandals because I had to go to this barbecue with Mom. All the delegates organizing for her were invited—it was a real mob. Tables were set up outside in the courtyard, and inside was a big spread of hamburgers and coleslaw. I stood by Mom while she gave her pep talk. I felt stupid and embarrassed and ridiculous the whole time. Why does she make me do it? I had to follow her around shaking hands and smiling and hardly had a chance to get more than a few bites of a burger. My hand still hurts from all those firm handshakes people just love to give. I think limp handshakes should come back in style.

Then Jonathan gave me leaflets to stick under doors—you know, pictures of Mom and her family and lots of cheerful chat saying how great she is. So I tramped up and down the hotel corridors with about five other kids until *that* was done.

Then it was time to go to the tribute to Croix, which was being held in the Saddledome. We had good seats right in the centre section but it was not something Mom was looking forward to.

Mom blames Croix for the fact that the Liberals lost the last election. She feels we could've won with a different leader and thinks he was really selfish to stay on because now we have four more years of the Tories to put up with. I think she's right. Although I must say he's always been very polite and nice to me, and when we met on Parliament Hill he showed me his office and everything.

The central podium was all done in red and there was a full orchestra in the pit. Up high in glass booths were CBC TV and CTV.

First the lights went down and there was this big movie tribute. Then aboriginal people came on stage in full formal dress and all the multicultural groups joined them, everyone dressed in costume. They sang a beautiful song about Canada and I must say it made me feel a little teary. I wasn't the only one. All the kids were wiping away tears. Then Croix came on and the crowd gave him a standing ovation. Mom and all of us had to stand up too, even though we didn't feel like it.

I guess the crowd liked his speech because people were on their feet clapping for most of it. I couldn't help but think that lots of it was half-truths and he was leaving out more than he was saying. Still, by the end something funny started to happen in my stomach. I could feel the excitement moving through the crowd like a wave. It started to sink in that he was leaving and in two days there'd be a new leader who could be the next prime minister. And I started to sense just how important all this is.

After the speech the Young People of the Calgary Stampede came on stage. They all wore red sweaters and white skirts or pants. They had a lead singer who was dressed in a white shirt and black skirt. They sang "Oh Canada Land of Promise" and the whole crowd got up and swayed back and forth together. It was pretty neat.

When it broke up, we all walked over to the corral for the rodeo. I've never seen a rodeo before. Mom has, and I know she doesn't like them, but she has to show up. Why doesn't she just come out and say it's cruel to animals if that's what she believes? I know why. She doesn't want to lose half the delegates from the West. Why can't adults ever just say what they think and be honest? They sure expect us to be completely honest about everything!

I look around for Paul but don't see him. We'll never find each other here. There are just too many people.

The lights dim and a rider shoots out of the pen and into the corral. It is announced as the Bucking Bronco event. I'd never imagined from seeing it on TV how really wild the horses are. I am immediately terrified that someone is going to get killed. The first guy out gets thrown but seems okay. The second guy gets his leg caught in the stirrup, and by the time he gets untangled he limps off the field. When that event is finished, the Rodeo Queens ride around on their horses, doing nothing except looking pretty, but they sure can ride. When they leave, these little kids come into the arena. Each one rides a sheep until they fall off. They are wearing helmets.

"Oh, they're cute!" I say to Lara.

"What if they fall off!" she replies, obviously upset. Then I get nervous too. One does fall and cries and won't be consoled.

". . . no business exploiting children like that," I can hear Mom say—but of course not loud enough for anyone but us to hear!

I had no idea bulls were so big. When the first bull comes out, with a cowboy on its back, my heart ends up in my throat. It runs and then stops very suddenly, pitching the cowboy forward. A clown gets between it and the cowboy while the cowboy gets up and away. Then two other cowboys on horseback head it back to the pens. Another bull comes out, bucking and heaving. Right in

69

front of us it throws off the rider who lands just behind it. The bull then kicks out its back legs and, with the most sickening thwack I've ever heard, kicks the cowboy in the side of the head. He falls down, gets up, and actually manages to run off with two other cowboys holding him up. But as I peer down the track, I see him collapse as soon as he's out of the corral. I feel sick.

"I need some fresh air," I say to Lara, that horrible sound still reverberating in my head. "Will that guy be all right?"

Lara shrugs. I turn to look at Mom. She looks kind of pale.

"You should say something," I accuse her.

"It's not so simple, Ali," she replies, bending towards me. "It's not just the delegates either. These cowboys love what they do. The danger is part of it. It's their choice."

I turn back to see that something is wrong with the bull. Its back half seems to be somehow paralysed and it is lying in the ring, unable to move. All the cowboys and a big first aid truck are running over to see if they can help. I get up.

"I'm getting out of here," I say.

"I'll meet you at the front entrance of the Roundup Centre, Ali," Lara says to me.

"What time?"

"It's nine-thirty now," Lara says. "How about eleven? If we want to stay longer after that we can, but let's meet then."

I nod and scramble out of our row. I wave to Mom and rush out into the corridor. I find a bathroom where I splash cold water on my face. Then I start to wander down the corral corridor, which is round of course, with entrances at intervals leading into the corral. Paul walks out of one of the entrances just as I get to it.

"Coincidence?" he grins. "Not exactly. It's not hard to spot your Mom, and I just kept an eye out for you. Saw you leave. Don't you like it?"

"It's so gross," I exclaim. "That guy got kicked by the bull right in front of me."

"Really?" Paul says. "We couldn't see that clearly from where we were sitting. They're still trying to get that bull into the wagon," he adds, gesturing.

"I think it's cruelty to animals," I state.

"The cowboys say the horses love it," Paul replies. "Who knows what the real truth is," he adds.

I look at him in surprise.

"What do you mean?"

"I mean it seems hard to figure out what the real truth is sometimes."

It looks like something is bothering him and it's not necessarily the rodeo.

"Hey," he says, "want to see my dad's trailers?"

"The famous James trailer?" I ask. "But I thought you weren't supposed to be seeing me."

"I'm not." He smiles. "But they're all inside and we're out here so who'll know the difference? I figure we've probably got fifteen minutes."

For a second I pause. Do I want to go to a trailer alone with him? I know the answer right away and the answer is yes. Maybe he'll try to kiss me. Or, I think, maybe I'll try to kiss him!

"Sure," I say. "Let's go. Oh, and Paul?"

"Yeah?"

"Happy Birthday."

9:30 P.M.

We are walking towards the back of the Roundup Centre. I am following Paul to his dad's trailer. My heart is pounding. What am I doing? Mom will kill me if she finds out. So will Lara. Not to mention of Dad and Mike, who come in tomorrow at suppertime. Oh man. Well, never mind. I console myself it's just as dangerous for Paul. Maybe I should show him Green House. But there are *always* people there, so I couldn't easily get away with it, whereas he swears his dad's trailer is empty.

"There are two trailers," he explains. "One is Dad's personal one where he can have meetings and rest up without rushing back to the hotel—it even has a shower. The other one is for his workers. They plot strategy there, give out pamphlets, organize."

"Convince Green delegates to desert by giving them pizza," I interrupt.

I think he's blushing.

"That's all part of the game," he says, sounding very defensive.

"Sounds like bribery to me," I retort.

"So I suppose your mother is perfect," he shoots back.

"No," I admit, "she's not. Well, none of them really say what they think, do they?"

He looks at me seriously.

"No, they don't." He kind of snorts. "If they did, they'd never get elected."

"Man," I say, "you sound even more down on it all than me."

"I'm not really," he says. "I might go into politics one day. But I'll be different. I'll be honest and say what I think and if I don't get elected . . . well, too bad. That's the only way to do it!"

"Good for you!" I exclaim. "Except," I add, "I'm not sure it's so easy. Mom is about the most honest person in the world, but she doesn't speak out the way she used to. And if she did, maybe she'd lose to someone who is just a good liar! It's so frustrating, it's so confusing . . ."

"Well, what about you?" he asks. "What do you want to do?"

I can hardly believe my ears. Someone actually wants to know something about me, not my mother.

"Don't know," I answer. "I'm good in science and math and I'll probably go into science. I wouldn't mind being a doctor but I hate the sight of blood. I almost threw up in the rodeo. Maybe I'll go into physics or be an astronomer. I like the stars and stuff."

Now I feel really embarrassed. Did I sound totally geeky? Why did I have to babble on like that?

"That's great!" he replies, and I relax a bit.

We have passed a number of people, some of them media types, but so far no one's taken too much notice of us. We go outside. It's dark out of course, but there are lights everywhere, so in fact it's quite bright. I see the two trailers dead ahead.

"Come on," he whispers.

I wonder why we are doing this. Of course I'm a little curious to see the trailer but I know that the real reason is so that we can be alone for a bit. There are steps leading up to the trailer. Paul takes them first. I hang back, looking around furtively. Paul opens the door and peeks in, then waves to me. I hurry up the steps and we close the door. He flips on a small light over a table in the kitchen.

"This won't show outside too much," he says.

"Wow, this is neat," I say. There's a living room, a kitchen. There are doors off the living room. Paul opens one door onto a tiny bathroom. He points to the beds, which are built in and pull out of the wall.

"Neat," I repeat.

"But not as big as Green House," Paul says.

"Yeah," I say, thinking about it for the first time, "I wonder how we got that and you got this and Heraux just gets a tent."

"Money, of course," Paul replies.

"Yeah, but where did Mom get all that money?" I ask. "We're certainly not rich. 'Course *you* are, aren't you?" Sure Ali, I say to myself, ask a really dumb question!

"Yeah," Paul says, not seeming to mind, "pretty much, I guess. I'm surprised you've never thought about the money part of all this," he adds, looking at me in genuine disbelief. "Money is *so* important."

"I've sort of tried to ignore the whole politics thing," I admit. "Whenever they talk about it at supper I just tune out,

75

and whenever Mom wants to tell me stuff, I basically tell her I'm not interested." I guess this must sound really weird to someone who loves politics. I try to explain. "See, none of my friends are into it, and they sort of make fun of me, and I've just tried to ignore it all. Like when I have a friend for dinner all everyone talks is politics. It's embarrassing."

"Shsh," Paul says. "What's that?"

He rushes to the door and peeks out the little window.

"It's Dad!" he hisses with horror. "And he has people with him. They'll be here in thirty seconds."

"We have to hide," I whisper.

"In there," he points and we both rush into the bathroom. As soon as the bathroom door shuts, the outer door opens and I hear Paul's father ushering everyone in. And I also realize how stupid we just were. If we'd just sat down at the kitchen table they might have been mad but it would've all been out in the open. If he comes into the bathroom and finds us alone in here . . . Oh my God, what a mess! I pray none of them needs to pee.

Paul and I are squeezed up against each other. At first it's so embarrassing I'm ready to die. But slowly he puts one arm around my waist, then the other so we're sort of hugging. I put my arms around his back. This is fabulous and exciting, and I start to hope we are stuck here forever. Romance in the toilet! I've completely forgiven him for last night. He's bossed around by his dad and there's not too much he can do about it.

"So gentlemen, I've heard rumours," James says, and it sounds like he's practically right beside us, "that our deal is the talk of the town."

"It's all rumour," says another voice. "There is *no* proof, Alex. I can promise you that. And as long as there is no proof, Green can't use it."

I stop breathing. I know we shouldn't be hearing this. Is this what Saul was talking about this morning? Paul, instead of letting me go, squeezes harder.

"At any rate," says the other voice, "here is the rest of it, as promised. Two hundred thousand dollars."

"Thanks, Frank," James says. "In a year, we'll be in government, and if I'm the leader I'll make sure you get to build not only the terminal but the new runway, too. If I have to move to Green on a final ballot, I'll insist on the transport ministry as part of the payment for sending my people to her. Don't worry. She'll agree—she'll have to. So either way, you're covered."

"Listen, Alex," says the voice, "we've never written down a word of this. Someone has obviously leaked from my office or yours, but it doesn't matter. As I said, with no proof, she can't say anything."

I hear another voice now.

"We've decided to beat her to it, just in case she tries to tip off the press," he says. "We'll accuse her of something tomorrow morning. She'll be so busy trying to defend herself she won't have time for this."

"Good," James says. "Let's get back to the corral, put in our last appearance for the night, then meet back at the hotel to work out how and what we're going to throw at Green tomorrow."

I can hear them shuffle off their benches. The door opens, then slams shut.

Paul had slowly loosened his grip the more we heard until by the time they left we were just two kids squashed together.

"I gotta go," I say, feeling numb but terrified. "I have to get out of here." What would James do if he found me? He's capable of anything. Murder maybe. No, that's silly. Isn't it?

I try to turn and I fumble with the door handle. Paul tries too until we spill out into the trailer proper. I can hardly look at him but I force myself. It looks as if he's crying. His eyes are all red. He sinks down onto one of the benches.

"Are you going to tell?" he says.

"I don't know," I find myself answering, and that's the truth. In one minute my entire world has turned upside down. I should tell, I know that. James is obviously a crook. And I should warn Mom that they're gonna attack her. But I look at Paul and I feel so bad for him. He'll be so humiliated. I go to sit with him and I take his hand.

"It's not your fault," I say gently. "He's your dad, not you."

Tears start to trickle down Paul's face. He pulls his hand away and puts his head in his arms to hide that he's crying.

"I hate him," he mumbles, "I hate him."

I don't know what to do or what to say. I feel so helpless. I try to pat Paul's shoulders. I wish I could tell Lara but if I tell her she'll tell Mom and that'll be that.

"Look, Paul," I say, "I promise I won't tell anyone anything yet. Maybe you and I can figure out something together."

He looks up, suddenly defiant and angry.

"Forget it, I don't need your pity." He pushes past me. "You probably think your mother is perfect. Well, if you aren't rich, where did she get over a million dollars to run her campaign? Think about that! Maybe she's no better than my dad!"

"Yes, she is!" I find myself yelling back. "She's lots better. She's honest."

"Oh yeah? And I suppose she *always* says what she really thinks." I remember the rodeo and how she wouldn't speak out on it and suddenly I wonder. I wonder about everything.

Paul opens the trailer door and without waiting for me runs down the steps and towards the Roundup Centre.

Great! I realize that if I'm caught here alone they'll think I'm spying or something. I run after him and catch up just as he gets to the door of the Roundup Centre.

"Paul!"

He stops.

"We don't have to fight."

He looks at me and all the anger crumbles away but I almost wish it hadn't because it's replaced by a look of sheer defeat. He seems crushed.

"No," he says, "we don't. But you won't want anything to do with me."

"Don't say that. Don't tell me what I'll want or won't want! You aren't your dad. Look, how about we go in and have a dance and try and calm down. Let's give everyone something to talk about. Paul James and Ali Green dance together at the rodeo."

I can see something in that . . . appeals to him.

"Yeah," he says, "let my dad deal with that!"

"Yeah, let your dad and my mom deal with it!" I say and we walk back into the corral hand in hand.

DAY 4

Friday, July 8

7 A.M.

"Ali, wake up! Ali!"

It's Mom's voice. I didn't see her last night. She didn't stay for the dance. I met Lara at the appointed time and convinced her to let me stay at the dance till it was over at one in the morning. Paul and I danced all night.

We had a really nice time. I keep my eyes closed for an extra second just to think about it. We fast danced and slow danced and talked and was it ever nice to talk to someone who's in the same boat as I am. I really like him. He's the first boy I've ever really liked. Maybe I'm in love. I'm sure old enough. Practically fifteen. So is he. I wonder if we'll ever get to be alone long enough to kiss!

"Ali, wake up, young lady!"

Uh oh. And why is Mom here? I open one eye a slit and moan.

"Whaaat?"

"What," she repeats. "What! I'll tell you what! Your picture, in a clinch with Alexander James's son, is plastered over the front page of every newspaper in the country."

Suddenly I'm very wide awake.

There *were* photographers everywhere even though I could see the organizer trying to keep the media out because they wanted people to be able to relax without worrying about cameras. This one big camera guy almost gave a volunteer a body check as he crashed past her into the corral. The media must've won 'cause by around ten they were all over the place.

"Let me see."

A newspaper is pushed in front of my face.

"Oh, how embarrassing," I mutter. "All my friends are gonna see this."

"Your friends," Mom almost screams, "never mind your friends!" She is actually angry. She's losing her temper! Wow. Well, I wanted to get her attention and I got it.

"No," I lash out at her, suddenly very wide awake and very angry too, "never mind my friends. Never mind them, never mind me, it's only you, you, you!"

"It's not me, Ali, it's the election, the country . . ."

"No," I say glaring at her, "it's you! You don't really care about me at all and this is a perfect example, isn't it? A normal mother would ask me about my date or the boy or if I like him or yell at me for being out too late but not you! You're not a mother, you're just a . . . a . . . a . . . politician! Oh, leave me alone. Where's Lara?"

"She's next door," Mom says. Then suddenly she sits down on Lara's bed in a kind of slump and looks at her feet. She's not dressed yet—she's in a big white terry robe and she has furry slippers on 'cause her feet are always cold. When she looks up, I'm shocked to see that she's smiling.

84

"Do you like him?" she says.

"What if I do?"

"Is he nice?"

"Yes!" I answer defiantly. And then I add, "Nicer than his dad, that's for sure!"

"What do you mean?"

Oh God, now what do I do? I mean, when I was with Paul I was sure promising not to tell was the right thing. But this is my mother after all. And if I don't tell her, James might get elected and he's a crook! And what is he going to throw at her today? Could he have anything on her? Is she as honest as I've always thought? Shouldn't I warn her? Then I remember what Paul said about money. I realize I *am* stupid not to know more, I should've listened at least some of the time instead of trying to change the subject the minute Mom talked politics.

"Mom," I say slowly, "how can we afford all this?"

"All what?"

"Everything. The campaign. It must cost lots of money. We aren't rich. Sometimes you take three plane trips a day. All the hotels you stay in, all the mail you send out to people. All the organizing. How does it get paid for?"

"Ali, I can't believe I'm hearing this. It's no secret. We've talked about it at home."

"I never listened."

"Why do you want to know now?"

Oh oh. Maybe I don't want to know.

"I just do."

"Your grandfather has had a lot to do with it."

"Zaida?" I say, really surprised. We see Baba and Zaida for a couple months every summer and at different times in the winter. They moved to Arizona when Zaida retired from his law practice. He went into business down there and did really well. He's flying in on Saturday for the vote. I like Zaida a lot. He reminds me of a very big teddy bear, all hugs and smiles. Baba is calm, like Mom.

"He's helped a lot," Mom says. "Also he's managed to get the big corporations he deals with in Canada to put in lots of large donations. It's those that've really kept the campaign going."

"Like what kind of companies?"

"Oh, insurance companies, a couple of banks, large manufacturers, that sort of thing."

"And why do they give money?" I ask.

"They hope you'll remember them when you're in government," Mom answers. "If there's a contract up for grabs or if there's government business and the government needs a bank to handle loans or to bail out a company, the people who've given you money hope you'll remember, and that you'll choose their company when the time comes. Or if you want to put in a piece of legislation and their companies or banks don't like it, they'll remind you that they helped you get elected and that they could help someone else next time. Actually, some of them give money to all the different parties at election time just to be on the safe side—that way no matter who gets elected they owe that company a favour."

It doesn't sound fair to me.

"Why don't they change the rules?" I ask. "Why do you have to spend so much money? What about someone who's smart but doesn't have a rich father with all these fancy business connections? Like without Zaida, *you* wouldn't be able to run."

"You're right, Ali," Mom says. "I had no control over this, but the first reform that needs to be made is a limit on spending. And I've pledged to do that."

"Will you pay them back?"

"I've told everyone: no promises, no pay-backs." She looks at me with a twinkle in her eye. "You know, honey, if I win I could be in a lot of trouble because they think I'm not serious when I tell them that."

"You could be in a lot of trouble," I agree.

"We'll cross that bridge when we come to it," she says. "For now, one step at a time." She pauses. She comes over and sits beside me on the bed. "I'm sorry I blew up. Of course you can see this Paul boy if you want. Just don't tell him any secrets and don't let me see you in a James T-shirt! Are you sure he's a nice boy, Ali? His father is . . . well, a pretty tough character. Some say he made his millions through insider trading. He'll fire an employee over nothing—he's ruthless."

"Paul's not like his dad at all! He's not! He hates his dad," I blurt out.

Again she pauses.

"I know it's . . . tough for you kids," she says. "We never see each other. You probably hate me half the time."

I don't correct her.

She sighs.

"Well, it'll be better if I win. Then we can all be together again."

"Yeah," I say throwing back the covers and stomping out of bed. "In Ottawa! I won't move. I'll stay in Winnipeg with my friends. You can't make me move!"

"Ali, now stop it. Kids move all the time if their father gets a new job. This is no different. Anyway, I'm not going to argue with you now. I'm really behind schedule."

I snort. "Talk to me for five minutes and it throws out your whole day. Anyway, you wouldn't have said two words to me if it hadn't been for those pictures."

"I'm sorry, Ali, I've said so. Just try to understand. This is something I want so badly. I don't want it at my family's expense, but it seems that I just can't do it all!"

I can see she's getting upset again now.

"Come next door for breakfast when you're dressed," she calls over her shoulder. "You can see the rest of the papers!" She's out the door before I can reply.

I go back to the bed and pick up the newspaper. The picture is taken from the side, we are talking as we dance. I am looking up into Paul's eyes with a goofy look of love and he is gazing into my eyes with what some could call gooey eyes. Oh man. Still, from that photo it looks like he really likes me. I don't know how I can face him today. In fact, how can I face *anyone*? Everyone in the world will've seen this picture. Everyone will tease me or be mad at me, thinking I'm a traitor, or think we're stupid. I take my time getting dressed in a clean and dry Green T-shirt and cut-offs. "Canada A.M." is on as usual. Just before the news, the announcers always chat for a second—and what do they talk about today? Me and Paul!

"So, the latest hot news item is that Paul James and Ali Green danced the night away."

Oh God! This is a nightmare!

We thought we'd get his dad upset, and I thought it might needle Mom a bit, but we really didn't think the papers would care. When a couple of flashes went off around us, I never dreamed any paper would print our pictures! I figured all the people there would gossip and talk but the thought of that was funny. This isn't funny. And what do I do about Mom and James? Actually, out-side of Lara, Dad's the only one I could really trust. Should I tell him? Or would he tell Mom? And without proof, would it do any good to tell? I really feel sick about this. I promised to meet Paul at the Leadership Forum this morning. I hope he's thought of something.

10 A.M.

When I walked into Mom's room, everyone teased me
mercilessly. Saul kept chanting, "Ali's got a boyfriend," just
like a little five-year-old. Lara just kind of looked at me and
shook her head. She's upset with me, I can tell. She thinks
this'll hurt Mom somehow. But the bigwigs didn't seem to
take it too seriously. I, on the other hand, was horrified.
Mom wasn't exaggerating when she said that our picture
was plastered over every paper in Canada. It was the same
photo, too, but with lots of different captions. The
Winnipeg Free Press had "Romeo and Juliet?" written
under it and the *Sun* had "Rodeo Romance!!" Oh! I'll *never*
be able to show my face in Winnipeg again. And the really
upsetting thing is that I can't even blame this one on Mom.
It was all my idea! Pay back his dad, eh? Great thinking.

I couldn't face the media in the lobby so I told Mom I'd
leave after her, and take a cab to the stampede grounds

myself. She had to go to the Westin Hotel for breakfast and give a talk to five hundred people.

I have a meeting at Green House at ten-thirty, then the Leadership Forum sponsored by the Aboriginal Commission at eleven. I wonder if that's where James plans to drop his bombshell on Mom. And I wonder what it is? I sat in my room for an hour trying to figure out what to do about James. I could tell Mom but then I'd have to explain going with Paul, alone, to his dad's trailer. I don't think that would go over very well. And if I do say something and Mom uses it, Paul will be humiliated forever by his dad being called a crook from coast to coast. I mean, I know what he'd have to go through. I can relate to it. It's bad enough being singled out all the time 'cause you have a famous parent. But what if that parent is famous for being a crook? Life at school would hardly be worth living. Kids use that kind of stuff against you and so do grown-ups. It's not fair. But it's not just that. He won't be able to hold his head up. When I met him, I thought he was very secure, but now I realize he's just as insecure and full of doubts as I am. I keep wondering what I'd want him to do if everything was reversed. Well, I know. I'd want him to keep his mouth shut.

On the way over to Green House, I try to steel myself for what is to come. I would've stayed in the hotel all day, but I promised to meet Paul.

Everyone teases me. When I go out to the grass in the back where our group meets, all ten kids start to clap and chant:

"Juliet, Juliet, Juliet!"

I'm too embarrassed to tell them to shut up, so Jonathan does it for me.

"I know, Ali," he says, "you're really spying for us, right? Tell us everything you found out! The dirtier the better!"

If only he knew.

Anyway, they quit razzing me after a while and we get down to more serious business. We have a lot to do today because tonight the candidates present their speeches in the Saddledome. My stomach lurches at the thought of it. It's the last big event before the voting tomorrow and the most important. I'm getting awfully nervous about Mom's speech. I know she's going to spend all afternoon on it today. It's important. It could ruin her chances if it's bad or she makes some major mistake. Lara told me that she doesn't think the speeches actually sway that many delegates the day before the vote, but in a close race, fifty or a hundred could mean the difference. Also it'll be on national TV—the whole country will be watching. If she wants to win in the next election, this'll be really important.

Each candidate gets to have a five-minute demonstration before the speech. We have to discuss that, and the seating strategy. Jonathan wants to be sure the Green Youth is seated right in the front of the stage, which will mean waiting at the Saddledome for hours so we can rush in to get good seats as soon as they open the doors. A rehearsal is planned for one o'clock, right after the forum.

Anyway, we get the details worked out and I decide to head over to the Roundup Centre. It's now ten forty-five, the forum starts at eleven, and I'm supposed to meet Paul in five minutes just at the entrance to Centre Hall. I notice people pointing as I walk and I wish I could disappear. I just hope that if I can make it through this morning the rest of the day won't be as bad. After all, how long will people be thinking about me and Paul with the vote only a day away? In fact, I can feel the atmosphere changing, getting more and more intense. The youth delegates are going everywhere in groups waving their placards. Animated conversations are happening everywhere, reporters are scurrying about, the whole place feels charged with energy. I get to our meeting place but Paul is nowhere to be seen. Waiting for him is horrible as I am getting lots of stares and whispers. I can only figure it'll get worse when he shows up and I'm starting to think that maybe I should just go in and get a seat with the Green troupe when an older kid, maybe eighteen, comes up to me and asks if I'm Ali. He's got a James T-shirt on. I nod. He sticks a note in my hand and walks into the room.

"I'm grounded in my hotel room till the speeches tonight. Sorry. Love, Paul."

Love, Paul. I read it over and over and over. Then I fold it carefully and put it in my pocket. Love, Paul. I walk through the crowd in a daze, automatically saying hello to people I know, until I find a seat. I sit down and put my hand in my pocket, fingering the note. My first love letter. I pause and think. My first love letter is a note that basically tells me I'll never see him again! This is just great. Maybe I should go to his hotel? But I have to be at the practice or I'll be missed and then I have to be with the kids to get seats. I don't think any of us will get back to our hotels. Someone is handing me a placard and someone else punches me on the arm. I look over and see Terry leaning towards me from two chairs away.

"Wake up, Cinderella! The ball is over and there's work to do!"

I try to punch her back but she moves out of the way.

Soon all the delegates are on their feet, clapping and cheering as the candidates move on stage. There are introductions by the aboriginal chairpersons and the usual description of how the forum will be run. I really can't concentrate so I just cheer when everyone around me does and sort of tune out. They start the debate and I sit here worrying about Paul. How much trouble is he in? Is he alone? I wonder if I could try calling his room?

94

Suddenly I am shaken out of my thoughts by booing which is coming from all around me. Now the crowd is on its feet screaming "Green, Green, Green." I put down my placard and squeeze over to Terry.

"What happened?" I ask. Everyone looks really upset.

"Honestly, Ali," she says over the hubbub, "get with it. That's the kind of scum we're dealing with. Do you have to make such *good* friends with his precious son?"

I am shocked by the vehemence in her voice. She really hates James.

"What happened?" I repeat. "I wasn't listening."

"James just accused your mom of being involved in a land deal in your riding in Winnipeg. He said your grandfather got a contract to build a big new sports facility and isn't it a coincidence that it's in her riding?"

"But Zaida builds stuff," I object. "He gets his own contracts. It has nothing to do with Mom!"

"Of course it doesn't," Terry agrees. "But by the time people figure that out, the damage will be done. Her whole platform has been honest, caring. If he can make her look as creepy as everyone else, he's won!"

I push back to my seat.

Mom is on her feet.

"I would like to make it quite clear," she says, "that my father is a successful businessman who was awarded that contract because his was the lowest bid. As my opponent well knows, we are not in government either at the provincial level or the federal level and therefore it is not me or our party which has anything to do with awarding contracts. When we are in that position, I will make it my business to make sure that no such thing happens." She waits for a minute. Everyone has sat down. There is a long silence. She speaks again.

"I am sorry that my opponent has felt it necessary to drag the debate down to this level. We are all Liberals, after all. We have to go on together after tomorrow. Our real enemies should be the Tories, not each other. I know that my opponent (why won't she say his name?) understands all too well that his accusations are groundless. I ask him to retract or bear the consequences."

James is sitting there, his face the colour of a beet. I guess he figured Mom would get all flustered and yell and scream and deny it so hard everyone would believe it was true. But she is so calm. Her voice is quiet, controlled. For the first time since all this started, I see that she is a natural leader. I feel really proud of her.

James clears his throat. "Ms. Green seems well versed with all the particulars," he concedes. "Perhaps I was a little premature in my conclusions. But," he says, getting his wind back, "you can never be too careful. She may castigate me for saying publicly what people have been saying privately for weeks."

"That's not true," I say to no one in particular. "No one's been saying it but *him!*"

"But she's not the only one that believes in honesty. Let's confront these issues. Let's get them out in the open!"

"James! James! James!" All his supporters are on their feet screaming. Then we get up. The chairpersons are trying to bring the forum back to order. After all, what has any of this got to do with aboriginal issues? Finally everyone settles down and the debate continues.

Just before one o'clock, Terry waves to me and a bunch of us leave to walk over to the Saddledome. I am so angry at James, I can barely contain myself.

"The papers will have a field day with this," Terry mutters as we walk. "I can just see the headlines—especially in the conservative papers. 'Green accused of back-room deals!' Stuff like that."

"It's not fair!" I exclaim. "How can people let him get away with it? Anyone can see he's lying. He practically admitted it in front of everyone."

"Yes," says Jonathan, "but the papers will sensationalize it, and what about all the delegates that weren't at the forum and didn't hear your mom's reply? That's what James is counting on. Sure he had to retract, but the media coverage will do a lot for him. It could give him the push he needs just before the election. After all, if people are voting for your mom on the honesty issue, and if he's just managed to muddy that . . . well. It could be enough."

I feel ill. I'm so mad I feel like going over there and killing him. I think of the note in my pocket. Well, I don't have time to spend half the afternoon tracking Paul down. Now I realize just how important it is to keep our vote from slipping and that I have to do everything I can to help. A little voice reminds me that only yesterday I didn't want her to win. That I don't want to move. Well, I'll deal with that later.

5 P.M.

We are so squashed together I can hardly breathe. I am standing in the foyer of the Saddledome, along with hundreds of other kids, waiting for the doors to open. It's been the craziest afternoon I can ever remember.

I almost went back to the hotel to talk to Mom a million times. But each time I had definitely decided to tell her, I'd stop myself by wondering just what I would accomplish. Would it help her to know this? How? I have no proof and there won't be any proof, James is too smart for that. She already knows he's crooked so I wouldn't be telling her anything new. And I'd be betraying Paul. After all, I gave him my word. I've never broken a promise to anyone and I sure don't want him to be the first. But what his dad did is so bad I still can't believe he did it. How can anyone be that dirty and sneaky? Actually, I thought it was only the Tories that had people like that in their party. I guess if there are creeps in our party, there might actually be a few nice guys in theirs. That's a strange idea.

It would have been difficult to get away at any rate because we were so busy all afternoon. Jonathan and a young woman called Leslie were in charge of the rehearsal in the Saddledome. We were the second group scheduled. James's people had already been practising and were mostly waiting around in the foyer. After us it was Potter's turn, then Baker, and finally Heraux. Jonathan took us into the centre of the arena and showed us the seats he wanted us to get. He perched on the edge of a chair and explained what would happen.

"Ros only has half an hour in all to speak and she says we can use five minutes—no more—for our demonstration. She wants to use the time for her talk, unlike some candidates, who shall be nameless," he grins, "who have nothing to say and therefore use lots of time for their demos. When it's our turn, you'll march onto the floor in front of the stage chanting 'We want Green,' waving your placards. Then we'll return to our seats. During the speech you'll be given a signal to let you know when to chant and how long to keep it up—and be careful, don't clap for too long because that all takes time away from her speech."

We practised for about an hour, just getting everyone in the right order and back to their seats quickly.

"Okay, everyone," Jonathan then called, "you can leave the dome until around four o'clock. By then the other groups will have finished their rehearsals. You'll have to wait in the lobby, so when the officials open the doors, you'll be first in line and can run down and grab seats." Personally, I think the organizers should have drawn lots or something to see who would sit where 'cause this is a crummy system—well, it's no system at all really.

Anyway, we were just gathering up our placards and getting ready to leave so the Potter team could practise, when the doors burst open and hundreds of James supporters rushed down the stairs and onto the floor to grab the seats in the centre just in front of the stage. They started pushing us out of the way and getting really rough. TV cameras materialized out of nowhere, as did a bunch of convention officials. One huge guy who I guess must be a university football star came right up to me and tried to grab the placard out of my hands. I fought with him and ended up with the stick end of it in my stomach for my trouble. Of course someone from one of the networks filmed the whole thing. I yelled at the James thug over the chaos, "You're making an idiot of yourself on national TV." He dropped the placard at that point and ran around breaking any Green placard he could find on the floor. We were under attack! The loudspeaker boomed and a female voice warned everyone that if the room wasn't cleared immediately, the entire evening event would be cancelled. Slowly the hubbub cooled, the James people left, and then so did we. But when we got to the foyer, we found the James people there. They explained someone had opened the door and they'd thought it was time to get seats. Great, I thought, is this what it'll be like when we have to rush for the seats? Jonathan and Leslie told us we'd better not leave after all, we were to wait in the foyer too, or the James people would beat us to all the good seats. That was around 2:30 P.M. and we've been in the foyer ever since.

After each of the other groups finished their rehearsals, they joined us and now it's so packed you can't even turn around. About an hour ago I had to go to the bathroom so bad I thought I'd die, so I spent fifteen minutes getting out, ten running to a washroom in the Roundup Centre, and another fifteen squeezing my way back through the crowd. I'd say I'm about in the centre of the foyer. Maria is near me and we chat. Around five minutes ago, juice boxes were passed out to everyone and now I can smell pizza. Yes, I can't believe it but people are passing boxes of pizza over heads to the crowd. I manage to get my arms up, grab a piece of vegetarian, and pass it on. I wonder who's paying for this? James is certainly famous for his free pizza lunches so maybe this is courtesy of him. Or maybe it's him and Mom. Anyway, although it's almost cold it tastes great to me. It's getting so crowded and hot that at times I feel really faint. How much longer till they open the doors?

I can barely lift my arm to look at my watch, my arm is so cramped. Six-thirty. My legs ache, my back hurts, I must smell, my hair is sticking to my neck. At least my Green T-shirt was clean this morning. I have the distinct feeling that everyone around me has been wearing the same T-shirt for days now. Mike and Dad must be here. Wonder if I'll get to see them. Probably not till tonight. At speech time, Jonathan wants me to leave the youth delegation and make my way up to the centre aisle where Mom, Dad, and Mike will be sitting. For the cameras—family unity and all that.

At least this is the last big event before the vote tomorrow. Of course, if Mom wins it'll just be one of the countless other events. If she wins. What will my life be like then, I wonder? Will I have the RCMP following my every move? I can just see it like a scene from some comedy—me on my bike and two guys in black suits and dark sunglasses trailing just behind me, on their bikes. Will they accompany me on dates? And what about the constant appearances on TV as I attend "functions" with Mom? And having to go on stage! In fact, I'll have to go on stage tomorrow if she wins.

In front of practically the entire country. I can feel the palms of my hands starting to sweat, just at the thought.

The crowd surges forward. Uh oh. This must be it. The doors are opened and I am propelled, almost off my feet, through the foyer into the Saddledome, down the stairs. At this point there is a huge rush for the seats but the James kids are way more aggressive. They grab all the centre seats on the floor before we even get there. We scramble for a block of seats just behind them and to the right. Heraux gets a block to the left, Potter higher up to the left, Baker higher up to the right. Once we have our seats, organizers hand out more placards. I look up to the media booths. They are filled with people being interviewed. Print reporters mill around the floor area. Not long after we're seated, delegates start to troop in.

I know Paul will be sitting with his family. There's a big dance tonight at the Roundup Centre. I wonder if he'll go? I wonder if he'll be allowed to see me again? Probably not. I try not to think about it, it's too depressing. Also I've been so cut off from the news all day that I have no idea what's happening. Did what James say cause a big scandal? Did Mom deal with it well enough? It's weird. We're surrounded by media, we're actually making news but we have no idea what's going on outside of this space.

Thousands of Green delegates and alternates and volunteers are cramming into the seats behind us here in the centre section. The James people can't all fit on the floor, of course, so now they have to split up a bit. They are over to the left, spilling around the Heraux group. Finally everyone is in, the chairpersons start the proceedings, and Baker is called upon to speak first. After him'll come Heraux, then Potter, then Mom, then James. That's just the way it happened when they picked the order out of a hat.

103

Baker gives a pretty boring speech, all he seems to do is yell. Heraux is next and he's actually funny—he slams the Tories for most of his speech. The crowd loves it and he gets a great hand at the end. They both have demonstrations before their speeches. Potter goes on and on about abortion, and me and my friends boo him. Now it's Mom's turn. My stomach is a mess of butterflies, that pizza is churning around in a very unpleasant way. We get up and march once around the floor screaming our heads off, waving our placards. I'm starting to lose my voice.

The demo goes well and I make my way into the stands. Mom's already on her way up to the stage. I'm so nervous for her I can hardly stand it. What if she completely blows it? I find Dad and Mike sitting beside Baba and Zaida, who arrived just in time for Mom's speech. Dad gives me a big hug and Mike, who sees how embarrassed I am, does the same just to bug me. They both have curly black hair and brown eyes and they're much taller than Mom and me. Zaida is famous for his bear hugs so I get another big hug from him. Thankfully, Baba just gives me a peck on the cheek. "How's my baby?" Zaida asks.

"Good," I reply. "Are you mad about what James said?"

"Mad doesn't describe how I feel, little one," Zaida replies. "But we'll rise above it, you'll see."

Mike has saved me a seat beside him on the end of the row. Lara is sitting beside Mike, Cathy and Saul are sitting right behind us. I can see everyone is really tense. The demonstration finishes—it seems like there are thousands up but I could be wrong. She'll need over two thousand votes to win. She starts to talk. She talks about all the things she wants to change—mainly how women and children aren't given any value in society and how that has to stop. She says she'll take money from big corporations and defence to pay for higher welfare payments, job training, literacy, abuse prevention and treatment, stuff like that. I feel very proud of her. None of the men talked about these things. I wonder if that means she'll lose? Then she talks about honesty and a different process of government, consultation instead of confrontation. And then she says that she'll continue to stick up for her beliefs even if it means some people get frightened and want to lash out at her because they are afraid she'll take away their chances for profit and, most of all, power. The crowd is on its feet. Everyone is screaming. Everyone knows she's just put James in his place and she did it so well! When the crowd quiets down, she continues. Her speech builds as she describes the country as it could be and the crowd is on its feet over and over, cheering and applauding. And at the end she talks about what democracy means. That it means listening to the people. And she promises that when her M.P.s come to her and tell her what their constituents want, she'll really listen. She won't say we're making tough decisions and of course people are unhappy but that's too bad. She'll listen to the people because *that* is democracy and sometimes it's messy but without the people we only have four-year dictatorships.

Finally it's over and amidst the screams and chants, she makes her way off stage, shaking hands. She comes and sits with us. Everyone congratulates her. Cameras are all around us. She's different, I have to say that!

The James people start their demonstration and then James gives his speech. His demo is large, very large. He's not a great speaker, I think he yells too much. He talks about money and responsible government and how his business experience will help him run the economy. He slams Mom indirectly by saying that without good economics all the social programs will suffer. Same old story. He doesn't mention the morning accusations.

Mike leans over to me.

"How's the little love bird?"

"Shut up!"

"Is he just like his dad?"

"No!"

"Going dancing with him tonight?"

"Maybe," I reply defiantly. Then I add, "What's in the news today about what James said this morning?"

"Well," he replies, "they're reporting it as an unfounded accusation along with Mom's denial. Frankly, I think even the media can see through this one. They don't like to be used and I guess they feel James is using them. It may cost him some votes in the end."

"Good," I say. "He's a pretty yucky character." I pause. "Mike?"

"Yes?"

"Oh, nothing."

"What is it?"

"Nothing."

"That's not what your face says."

"Shsh! Mom'll hear. Nothing."

"I hope you're not hiding something. Has Paul told you anything we should know? Because we could use all the help in the world right now."

"Why?"

We are whispering, covering our mouths so the cameras can't read our lips or the powerful media mikes pick up our voices.

"I hear she's slipping. This thing this morning didn't help and Heraux is picking up strength. I think people are shying away from electing a woman. Plus he's gaining some of James's delegates from Quebec." He pauses. "There's no way we'll win on a first ballot," he continues. "And then it could get good and messy."

I am so close to telling him. I want to. But what good would it do? Still, maybe Mom and her advisors could think of a way to use it. I've got to find Paul. I've got to get him to agree to let me tell. If only I had proof. I look at all the reporters swarming around us, cameras at the ready, mikes outstretched. If only I'd had one of those little tape recorders on me last night. And then the germ of an idea starts to form in my head. And for the first time since last night I start to feel like maybe, just maybe, I can do something to stop James. I look over at where James's family is sitting. Paul is there, of course, I'm sure, although it's too far away for me to see him. I have to meet him later. But how? How?

10 P.M.

The speeches are over, the demonstrations are over and I'm on my way to the Roundup Centre to see if I can find Paul. Of course I'm worried about Mom and about my promise to Paul. But I also can't help thinking that this could be our last chance to dance together or to be together at all.

What an event the speeches were. The chairpersons announced the number of people there—something like forty-five hundred delegates, five hundred observers, and thirteen hundred media. Then if you add in the honorary delegates, I'll bet there were almost seven thousand people in that arena tonight. The excitement level was phenomenal. At the end, everyone said Mom gave the second-best speech, after Heraux. Which is too bad because he's really getting strong.

Terry, Maria, and I are going to the dance together. Oh

yes. And Mike. He took one look at Terry and proclaimed that he'd have to go along to chaperon his little sister. Ha! I think a lot of the guys just see this as a great place to meet girls. Not Mike, of course. He's too much of a political fanatic to be that shallow. However, he does seem to be struck dumb by Terry.

Mike buys us tickets. "Dad gave me the cash," he whispers to me.

"Oh phew," I exclaim, "for a minute there I thought you'd lost your mind and become generous!"

He winks at me and ushers me into the room. We wait just inside the door for Terry and Maria as they get their tickets. There is a band playing at one end of the huge room and at the other is a long bar that runs the width of the space. There is an area for dancing near the band, then lots of round tables. It is already getting crowded.

"Will Mom come?" I ask.

"She'll put in an appearance to shake hands in a few minutes," Mike says. Then he slaps me on the back so I almost fall over. "And what about your boyfriend? Will he be coming?"

"Even if he does, how will I ever find him?"

The room is at least half a city block long and equally wide. It's not easy to find one person in a crowd of two or three thousand.

Something in my voice must startle Mike and for the first time since he's arrived he talks to me as if I could, just possibly, be a human being with feelings, not simply some twerpy kid sister.

"Hey, just don't tell him any state secrets and I'll help you find him," Mike says.

"You've never met him," I say. "You won't recognize him."

"I have met him. When I was in Ottawa once visiting Mom."

He just stops there. Doesn't add anything.

"And?"

"He seemed okay to me," Mike shrugs. "Tell you the truth, I didn't pay much attention to him."

Inwardly I heave a sigh of relief. If Mike wants to make my life miserable over this he can do it easily, but I get the sense he's decided against it for some reason. I know he hates James so I'm not sure what that reason could be.

" 'Course," Mike continues, "James also seems very nice on the surface. But things, or people, aren't always what they appear to be."

Uh oh. Maybe I relaxed too soon.

"What makes you think," he says, "that Paul isn't just like his father—he could be putting on a great act." Mike asks.

Terry and Maria join us.

"Who's putting on an act?" Terry asks.

"Why me, of course," Mike smiles at Terry. "I only pretend to be suave, debonair, brilliant, caring, and sensitive. Really I'm a political junky and you know what *that* means!"

Terry laughs.

"Ruthless," she says, "single-minded, opportunistic . . ."

"Stop, stop!" Mike pretends to weep. "You know me too well!"

Is this called flirting? It sucks.

I grab Maria's arm.

"Will you two excuse us, please?"

"We'll grab a table near the front, on this side, Ali," Mike calls after me. "Find us later. I'm to escort you home tonight!"

I wave in agreement and quickly propel Maria through the crowd.

"What a jerk," I mutter.

111

"I think he's pretty cute," Maria says. "If only I were two years older!"

"Looking for me?"

I feel a hand on my shoulder.

"Paul!"

Oh, that's good. Maybe I could scream louder and let the whole world know how happy I am to see him.

"How did you find me?" I chatter away. "I thought we'd never find each other. I have to talk to you. It's really important."

"I know, I know," he nods. "I've been waiting by the central door and I had a friend at each of the other doors in case you went in there," he says. "I didn't want to catch you when you were with your brother so I just leaned on the other side of that pillar until you split off from him." He looks around like a wanted man. "We can't talk here. My hotel room is 905. Meet me there as soon as you can get out of here."

"Are you nuts?" I say. "I'm supposed to be here with my brother."

"I can't be seen with you, Ali," Paul insists and he looks really upset. "This'll be our last chance to, to . . . talk."

Maria is sticking to me like glue, meanwhile.

"Bring your friend if you want," Paul says. "Just come. We can be back here in an hour without anyone really missing us."

I know he's right. If we try to talk or dance here, we'll soon have journalists all over us.

"Okay," I agree. "Room 905. In half an hour."

"And I'll be there, too," Maria pipes in.

"Great. Great," and he disappears into the crowd.

The music is really loud now, good rock and roll and I feel so sad that Paul and I can't just enjoy it together.

"Please don't tell Mike," I beg Maria. "He'd never let me go."

"Leave it to me," she says.

We find Mike and Terry dancing.

"We're meeting with some Winnipeg delegates at Green House," Maria shouts over the music. "Back in an hour!"

"Do you need me to come?" Mike asks. "Is it serious?"

"No, no," Maria assures him. "Just last-minute instructions for tomorrow."

She pulls me away before he has time to say anything else.

"Boy, Maria," I say as we hustle through the crowd. "How'd you get to be such a good liar?"

"Very strict parents," she replies, in a perfectly serious voice. "I love doing stuff like this," she adds.

She hustles me into the hallway where we run straight into Lara and behind her, Mom, Dad, and about fifty screaming supporters waving placards shouting "We want Green!"

My heart drops down to my feet.

Lara grabs me and shouts, "Where's Mike?"

"He's in there," I answer. I've been turned around now and am walking back in with them. Lara produces tickets, which she gives to the people at the door. The crowd stacks the placards in one place and begin to file in as well. Guess Mom will just shake hands, then leave, and the rest will stay and party. I break free from Lara.

"Gotta go to the bathroom. See you in a bit," I gasp, amazed at my new-found ability to lie. I've never done anything like this before. Never. I wouldn't do it now either except I have to talk to Paul. Then a horrible thought hits me. That's probably what James says to himself when he lies or takes bribes.

He probably says, "I have to in order to get elected, and then I'll be such a good leader how I got there won't matter."

113

But, I think, maybe it does matter. Maybe it starts to change the way you think. Oh stop it, I tell myself, what are you, Miss Goody-Goody? You've never told a little white lie before?

Maria and I are running down the corridor now towards the main doors. I start to feel yucky. What if I get caught? What if a reporter sees me going into his hotel? That would make great news coverage on election day. I could ruin it all for Mom.

I stop just before we reach the doors.

"I can't, Maria," I say.

"What?"

"*I can't.*" I turn and head back down the corridor. In front of me, almost running, is Paul, obviously heading for the central doors and a taxi.

I run up to him and grab his arm. A few people are milling about but no one really notices us. I motion for him to follow me through the doors.

"Change in plans," I call to Maria, letting her know that I want her to get lost. "I'll see you back at the dance."

I push the doors open and hurry out into the July night, heading for the grassy area where the pancake breakfast was held. Paul follows. There are quite a few people walking about, but no reporters and we move towards a group of large trees. I slip down on the ground and rest my back against a tree trunk. I motion him down beside me. It's quite dark here and I feel we can huddle without being noticed.

"Sorry," I say. "I just couldn't take a chance on getting caught going into your hotel. Also," I add, "I don't want to start lying to Mom and Mike and everyone. Once you start where do you stop?"

Paul settles in beside me, leaning against the tree. Our shoulders touch and once again I feel an electric current shoot through me.

114

Paul's next words sort of break the spell, though.

"Oh, aren't we little Miss Perfect?"

I am shocked. He sounds so bitter and so aggressive. Just like his dad. Could Mike be right? What do I know about him anyway?

"You think it's okay to lie just 'cause it's for a good cause?"

Paul snorts.

"If your parents are involved—definitely yes."

"That's just what Maria said." I think for a moment. "Maybe I'm being a wimp. Maybe you're right."

I can feel Paul turn to look at me. I look at him. I know what's going to happen. I know and I don't want to stop it. I want it more than anything in the whole world. I lean towards him. He bends his head. We kiss.

It's a long slow kiss that gets longer and soon my arms are around his neck and his arms are around my back and I don't want it to stop, ever. When we do stop, we gaze at each other and I try to read his expression in the dark. His eyes seem to glitter and he looks happy. I probably look like a goofy idiot, myself. This must be love, I think. What else could make you feel this way?

"Maybe," I say slowly, "the hotel isn't such a bad idea."

"No, you were right," he whispers, taking my hand. "It was a crummy idea. With my luck, Dad probably would walk in on us again." He pauses for a moment. "What are you going to do?" he asks.

"I don't know what to do," I answer. "I don't want to get you in trouble, I don't want you to have to deal with everyone knowing what your dad did. Anyway, I have no proof. But—well, I do have this idea."

"What?"

"I can't tell you."

115

"Why not?"

He is holding my hands in his. His hands feel so good—warm and strong.

"Because if I tell you, you might feel you have to tell your dad and I don't want you to have the same problem I've had. I've decided not to tell Mom but at some point you might see me talking to your dad. Just do something for me—back me up. Don't tell him I'm lying. I've thought about it a lot and I hope this is the best solution."

"I thought with all your talk about people being honest and speaking out, you would go right to your Mom or even the papers with this story," Paul says.

"Yeah," I sigh, "you'd think so. Everything used to seem so clear, so black and white. It doesn't anymore."

Paul sighs too.

"What?" I ask.

"Nothing is ever simple," he replies slowly. "Since we've been here and Dad's been parading me everywhere like a prize show dog, I've realized that's all I am to him."

I start to protest but Paul won't let me.

"No listen, it's true. I know I sound like I'm exaggerating, making it worse than it is, but I'm not. Basically Mom and our housekeeper have brought me up. My Dad and Mom are out at functions almost every night. I know it's not like this for most other kids whose parents are in politics. Their parents make time for them—even if it's not as much as they'd all like. It's just Dad. His career comes first. I come last."

He sounds so bitter. I feel terrible. What can I say? That it isn't true? It sounds like a pretty accurate description to me. I know I resent Mom a lot both for *not* being there and for being too overprotective when she *is* there. Still, somehow I also know she loves me and I guess listening to Paul makes me realize that things in our family aren't as bad as I

116

thought they were. I'm sure Paul's father loves him, but Paul has no way of feeling that. And maybe, just maybe, Paul's right and his father really doesn't care about him at all. That's a horrible thought.

"Anyway," Paul continues, "I figure I don't owe him anything. He's a crook. But part of me still loves him, I can't help that, and part of me hates him, too. Still, I don't know if I can back you up when it comes to the crunch, Ali, I have to think more. I don't know what to do. I mean, even after I say all this and everything, he's still my dad."

"Yeah, I know," I say. "I'll do what I have to do for Mom and you'll have to decide then. *If* I get a chance. I may not get a chance to do anything."

He changes the subject by kissing me again.

"Great dance music in there," he murmurs.

"You aren't serious?" I say, breaking out in a large laugh.

"I am serious," he says. "How upset was your Mom?"

"Really upset."

"When my dad grounded me, it was the most attention he's paid me in years. But he can't ground me tomorrow. And frankly, I don't see how it can hurt either of them. In fact, I think it'll help—give them some good publicity."

"Will your dad be there?" I ask.

"No, he's gone back to his room to huddle with advisors. Your mom is there now."

"Right. Let's wait another five minutes. Then she'll be gone. I'd love another dance."

We have five minutes to kill so there's no use wasting it. We spend it kissing.

Finally Paul pulls me up.

"Slow dance, too?" he asks.

"For sure," I reply.

And we go to the dance, hand in hand.

117

DAY 5

SATURDAY, JULY 9

7 A.M.

I lie in bed, eyes closed, and go over last night, again and again. It was quite dark on the dance floor, and very crowded and very noisy. I guess we got some stares and created a bit of a scene but everyone was bent on having a good time and they really didn't pay too much attention to us. We danced for at least an hour before an aide of James's came and almost physically pulled Paul off the floor. I guess it took that long for the news that Paul and I were at it again to get back to his dad and for him to send someone to retrieve Paul. But it was a great hour. We fast danced and he's a pretty good dancer. We slow danced and that was the best. The best. I've never felt anything like that before—when we were pressed up against each other, I felt like every nerve in my body was on fire. All I want is to be with him and instead I'll probably never see him again after today—if I get to see him at all.

On the other hand, if Mom wins and we move to Ottawa, Montreal is only two hours away by bus. And didn't Lara say James's family would be moving to Ottawa after the next election? What am I thinking? I don't want to move—not even for Paul! Do I?

These thoughts bring me back to earth with a thud. The first election we have to win is the one today, and how am I going to stop James? I can hear the shower. I turn over to see that Lara already has her clothes laid out—a very smart green suit. She hustles out of the shower and attempts a smile but I can see she's pretty upset.

"What's the matter?" I ask.

"James *and* Heraux are picking up delegates from us," she replies. "We're not sure we can pull it out. We're talking to Heraux's advisors now about a possible deal—if he gets more votes, your mom will throw her support to him. If she gets more votes, he'll tell his delegates to vote for her on the next ballot."

"And?" I say.

She sits on her bed.

"I've heard that Heraux has been talking to James about a deal."

"He might go to James?" I cry. "I don't believe it. It's just a rumour."

"Could be. Or it could be true. Depends what James is ready to promise him."

"But Mom likes Heraux. Why can't she promise him what he wants?"

"He wants finance and your Mom wants De Silva at finance. She wants Heraux for external affairs."

"But," I say, "external affairs is important—he shouldn't be mad about that."

"He wants finance," Lara repeats. She gets up and starts to dress.

"Who wants transport?" I ask, wondering if James has made that a condition in any of these negotiations.

"Transport?" she says, surprised. "I'm not sure. Transport isn't exactly a cabinet post anyone would want."

"No," I realize, "it isn't, is it?" James probably wouldn't ask for it—he just said that to those men to get their money. Once he was prime minister, he could award that contract by instructing whoever was in the post to do as he said.

"Lara," I say, choosing my words as carefully as I can. "Would Mom put James in her cabinet if she won?"

"She'd pretty much have to," Lara replies.

"Why?"

"Well, if she ignored him, all the people that love him and have supported him would get mad at her—that would split the party badly. No, she'll have to offer a cabinet post to everyone in the leadership race and a few who stayed out and gave her their support."

Oh, great, so he wins either way. And he'll make sure he gets a cabinet post where he can pay all his friends back. And then, if he's found out, everyone'll think Mom's whole government is crooked—especially after all her talk about honesty and stuff.

"It makes me so mad," Lara bursts out. And she actually kicks the bed, I can't believe my eyes. "Your mom is the only one who is talking about issues. She's the only one that isn't running on personality. Not," and here her old sense of humour rescues her, "that she doesn't have one, Ali, she does! But the others are running on image. She stands for something. She's told people about her policies. If Canadians don't stop electing people because of their per-sonalities and if they don't start making the people they

123

elect really represent them, what kind of democracy will we have? Look what happened to that Conservative M.P., when he voted against the G.S.T.. They threw him out of the party—and all he was doing was representing his constituents. Is that democracy? Is it?"

I guess she expects me to answer.

"No, Lara, it isn't."

"Okay," she says, "tirade over. By the way, have a nice evening?" She actually smiles.

"Yeah."

"What's he like?"

"Not like his father!"

"Okay, okay," she laughs. "Maybe I was a little hard on you. Actually he seems very nice."

"Thank you," I reply. I pause. "I really like him."

She sits on my bed and looks down at me. "No kidding."

I can feel myself blush.

"I picked the perfect guy, didn't I?"

"Well," she says, messing my hair with her hand as she gets up and continues to get ready, "I don't know why you say that. He's the son of your mom's biggest enemy, he doesn't even live in Winnipeg, and I hear he's been forbidden to see you! Sounds perfect to me."

"Where did you hear that?" I exclaim, throwing off the covers.

"I have my sources. Don't you two talk? Didn't he tell you?"

"Yes, we talk," I say defensively. "Of course we talk. But I guess he didn't want to tell me more stuff about what a jerk his dad is."

"More stuff?" Lara asks.

Uh oh. Bad slip. First Mike, now Lara. I have to be really careful what I say.

"Well," I explain, "I mean, just general parent stuff, you know."

124

"Ali," Lara says, "Mike thinks you know something. If you do, you should tell us. It could be important. Don't decide for us if it's worth telling or not."

I don't reply. I just go into the shower.

"Ali."

"Yeah, I know, Lara," I shout. "I'll meet you in Mom's room."

How did they get onto me?

I shower, do my hair, throw on my jeans and a clean Green T-shirt Lara has left out for me, and go to Mom's room. My zit, thank God, has dwindled to manageable proportions and I can completely hide it now with my cover-up.

The group around the table is bigger this morning. All the papers have headlines like, "Too close to call." "Race to Wire." A couple have small follow-up blurbs about Paul and me, but that story has lost interest compared to the big vote today. Mike is there, and of course, Dad. And Baba and Zaida. Baba fusses over me and insists on hearing all my news. She praises me over my report card and Zaida presses a ten dollar bill into my palm. Actually, Mom gave me fifty at the beginning of the week, most of which I haven't spent, so I'm coming out of this week richer, if nothing else.

"I hear you didn't get a grade below B," he grins.

"Thanks, Zaida," I say.

"Keep up the good work!"

"I will."

Mike comes up and messes my hair. Jerk.

"Have a nice evening, brother dear?" I ask.

"Yes," he answers, "and longer than yours."

"Creep."

Dad comes up and puts an arm around me.

125

"Maybe moving to Ottawa doesn't seem quite so terrible now."

"Don't count on it," I reply, not willing to let anyone off the hook just yet.

The room is getting crowded with people. Mom has coffee and cups and croissants out. Everyone is talking, drinking coffee, reading the papers.

"The *Regina Leader-Post* and the *Calgary Herald* came out for James," Mike tells me. "So did the *Globe and Mail* and the *Toronto Sun*. But the *Winnipeg Free Press* came out for Mom," he continues, "and so did both Vancouver papers."

"The rest?" I ask.

"Oh, they just gave pros and cons for each candidate without really endorsing anyone. What are you up to today?"

"I have to meet my group at nine. We're planning demonstrations during the vote and we're supposed to talk to as many delegates as we can today to try to stop any more from leaving." I pause. "It's so crowded here. Want to go to the coffee shop for breakfast?" I find the thought of a hot meal, pancakes in fact, irresistible, even if it means eating with my brother.

Mike agrees. Of course, the coffee shop is also very crowded—it is packed with people and there is a high buzz as people talk, laugh, exchange anecdotes, and get ready for the big day ahead. Mike and I can hardly eat, so many people come up to the table to wish us luck and to shake hands.

He does manage to make me feel really bad in the short time we do get to talk, though.

"Ali," he says, "I *know* something is up. I just know it. Paul has told you something I'll bet, and you won't tell us."

"That's stupid," I react—a bit too quickly. "You're just fishing. You think that he's bound to have let something slip and you're trying to weasel it out of me. Well, stop

126

fishing. Paul didn't tell me anything." That's technically true, anyway.

"No, little sister, I'm not just fishing, I can tell. You *want* James to get in? He could, you know. He really could."

I gulp down the rest of my pancakes, swig back some orange juice, and then push back my chair.

"I've got lots of work to do today," I say. "When they start to announce the results, I'll come up to the stands and join all you guys. See you."

I take off before he can grill me any more. I'd be sure to crack. And there still doesn't seem to be anything I can do. *If* Mom wins I can warn her off giving an important cabinet post to James—but what if that's the only way she *can* win? If I tell her now, she'll never agree to his demands, and instead of him throwing his support to her, he could cut a deal with Heraux. Then she'll have no say in *anything*. Oh man, what a mess. If only Paul and I could spend some time really talking, maybe we could figure it out together. As it is, it looks like what I do or don't do could decide who's going to lead this country after the next election. Now there's a scary thought.

1:30 P.M.

My stomach is not doing too great. Those pancakes have been sitting like a giant glob in my gut all morning. I'm so nervous my hands are practically shaking. This is it. The voting will soon begin.

I am with a couple of hundred other youth delegates lined up outside Green House, waiting to march together to the Saddledome. We'll go in chanting. I spent the morning with Terry and Maria, giving out Green pamphlets and talking to every delegate we could find. We found the Portage Interlake kids and tried to talk them into switching back—one of them agreed. Well, it could be the one vote we'll need.

At our meeting, Jonathan instructed us to be very careful about what we say today and who we say it to. He reminded us that at the NDP Convention, the CBC had these incredibly sensitive mikes that picked up everything and that they also had certain candidates wearing hidden mikes. He warned us to check that anyone we spoke to wasn't bugged and to always cover our mouths when we talked so the cameras couldn't read what we were saying. At the NDP Convention, the whole country got to hear the backroom deals that were made between the candidates.

Too bad, I thought, I didn't have a TV crew with me the other night.

The march starts. It's very slow. Everyone is yelling "First ballot, first ballot," but it doesn't look like we have a chance to win on the first. I, of course, am just as confused as ever. On the one hand, I'm dying for Mom to win 'cause she's the best and I'd be closer to Paul. On the other hand, I still feel really upset about leaving Winnipeg and all my friends. And I wonder if I'll get a chance to do anything before it's all decided in a few hours.

It's very hot out and the sun beats down on us as we move along the sidewalk towards the Saddledome. We all have placards to carry and they seem to be getting heavier by the minute. My stomach is getting worse and my head feels like someone has twisted a vice around it. Finally we're up the steps and into the Dome. We rush to get seats and manage to get a block together on the left-hand side. The James kids are already on the floor. They have formed a circle in the centre and aren't letting anyone break it. They are screaming one chant after another, waving their placards. How do they always manage to get the best spots for the TV cameras? The chairperson announces that everyone is allowed five minutes to demonstrate. Five thousand people get to their feet and start to yell for their candidate. There are these guys in suits and Green hats— they have long poles with electronic messages at the top and they flash them with Mom's name when they want us to yell. I guess they'll be directing the "spontaneous" demonstrations throughout the day.

The chairperson announces that voting can begin. Soon lines along the floor are six deep, and even the James delegates have to give way for voters. I find Maria and Terry. We wait together for an hour with about fifty others, screaming our lungs out: "First ballot, first ballot." Then finally we decide to go and vote. Just when we get to the floor, we run into an incredible mob.

"What is it?" I ask Terry.

"Trudeau," she replies.

And sure enough, there he is, our former prime minister right in front of us, going to vote. It seems everyone in the place wants to shake his hand. We follow in the wake of the mob and finally get to vote. I place my X beside Green and experience my very first vote that will really count. Of course, I voted for my friends Susan and Martin for school president and vice-president last year, because Susan promised to have more interesting theme days and better dances, but I must admit this feels *quite* different.

We gather with the rest of the Green kids who are still chanting, clapping, and rocking to the music that blares from the loudspeaker. When the chairperson finally comes to the mike to declare voting over, it's already four-thirty. I'm getting hungry. I realize I haven't eaten since breakfast. I decide to go out to the concession stand and get a hot dog and a drink. Terry and Maria come with me.

"How long before they announce the vote?" I ask Terry.

"At least an hour," she replies, "maybe two."

"Want to come up to where Mom is sitting?" I ask, knowing Terry would probably love to see Mike.

"Sure," she replies.

Maria wants to come too, so we troop up the stairs to the

upper middle section where Mom is seated with her advisors, plus Dad and Mike, Zaida and Baba. Mom looks pretty calm, all things considered. Dad, on the other hand, looks terrible. He's obviously been pulling his hand through his hair the way he does when he gets nervous and it is practically standing up on end.

"Dad," I smile at him, "your hair."

He immediately knows what I mean, and he pats it down the best he can. We are surrounded by TV cameras and mikes and really can't talk freely. Is this what it'll be like if Mom wins? I notice some very serious-looking guys sitting around us and I figure they must be plainclothes RCMP. Is that any way for a teenager to grow up? I wish it were all over and we were safely back in Winnipeg. Heraux should win. He'd be almost as good as Mom, James would lose, we wouldn't have to move, and I could still visit Paul lots whenever I go to Ottawa to see Mom. Maybe in a few years we could even go to the same university—Carleton for instance, so we could be together.

Everyone chats and tries to fill time. Zaida has a stream of people coming and going, as he talks to everyone. We wait. Mom goes over her acceptance speech, hoping she'll get to use it. Lara comes up from the floor.

"We need some demonstrations," she says. "We don't want our strength to flag for the second ballot."

"Don't talk second ballot, Lara," Mike insists.

She smiles. "Sorry, Mike. I think you and Terry and Maria and Ali should get down on the floor and put some spark into the kids."

Dutifully we troop down the steps to the floor where Jonathan is waiting for us. The James kids have once again formed a square in the centre of the floor, delegates on the inside and running backs on the outside. We couldn't get through that without major blood being spilled. So we send runners up to the stands. They tell all the youth delegates to meet on the floor for a demonstration. And we start. We march around the James delegates waving our banners, yelling, "Let's go, Green, let's go!" over and over. My voice is hoarse by now from all the yelling, but somehow I find the last bit left and scream as hard as I can. My arms ache from carrying the placards, but I realize that I can't let down now. None of us can. The James kids start to yell in response, and soon the other camps join in until the entire Dome is once again a screaming mob. For a moment I catch sight of Paul; he is leading a cheer inside the James cordon. He sees me, too. But we haven't even time to acknowledge each other before I march past and he's lost in the crowd. My stomach wrenches when I see him and I mentally kick myself. I really did it this time. Out of all the guys here I pick him, the worst choice in the world, for my first real boyfriend. How stupid can you get?

6 P.M.

The chairpersons have walked onto the stage twice now but both times were just for announcements. I got so nervous I could hardly stand it. Now they are back. I am sitting with Mom, Dad and Mike, Zaida and Baba. Mary Strong, the M.P. from the Northwest Territories is about to open the envelope. She does so. She starts to read.

"Total number of ballots cast—4,600. The number needed to win—2,300. Baker—156." His supporters jump up and cheer. "Potter—393." His supporters leap up and cheer. "Heraux—1,278." A huge crowd jumps up clapping and screaming. My heart is in my mouth. I can hardly breathe. If Mom's name is next, it could be all over. "James—1,331." The James delegates are up; they are screaming so loud I can barely hear the next figures. "Green—1,442." Mom shows no emotion, but everyone around us is on their feet screaming. Still, I have a feeling this is not what we were hoping for. I lean over to Mike, put my hand over my face, and ask him.

"What does it mean?"

"It's not good," he replies, "but it's not a disaster either. It's much lower than we hoped for—we were hoping for at least fifteen hundred to start so we could win on a second ballot. This means that it'll go to three ballots for sure and on that third ballot, who will give up? We need either Baker or Potter to come to us now, and we have to hope Heraux will drop out and come to us, too. But I don't think he will."

"Well, Potter'll never come to us," I say.

"I know, but he may not go to anyone. His vote might split evenly between James and Heraux, which is better than all of them going to James. None of them will come to Mom 'cause of her pro-choice stand."

Suddenly Mom's advisors are gone. I can see they are all over the floor talking to people from Potter's camp and Baker's camp. People will vote again in about half an hour so if any moves are to be made, it has to be soon. Mike leaves to go down to the floor, too; I decide to go to the bathroom. By the time I get back, everyone is huddled around Mom. Mike is there, too, so I ask him what's happening.

"Neither Baker nor Potter is staying in. They've both declared they're out and that their delegates are free to go where they want, but Potter himself says he's going to Heraux because Heraux is personally anti-abortion, and Baker is going to James."

"Oh no," I say with a groan.

"Oh yes," says Mike. "But," he adds, "don't give up hope. The media are making lots of it but I don't think all of their delegates will go with them. We'll pick up more than people think."

Mary Strong announces that voting is to begin and once

again lines form six deep on the floor. I stay put for a while then go down to vote. I wonder how long we'll be here for? Maybe like in the twilight zone, we'll never get to leave.

It's eight P.M. before we finish voting and the votes won't be counted for hours yet. Again we're ordered to the floor for another demonstration. And again I catch sight of Paul. This time he motions to me. I can see he's pointing to an exit on the far left side of the Dome. I give my placard to Maria and tell her I desperately have to pee, then I fight my way over there through the mob, the noise, the rock and roll on the P.A. There is no privacy, and when I meet him a ton of people mill around us, many eyeing us suspiciously.

"Hi," he says, and suddenly seems very tongue-tied.

"Hi."

"I had a great time last night."

"Me too."

"Maybe we'll see each other in Ottawa."

"Who do you think'll take it?"

"Could be Dad," he says. "They say he has the momentum."

"Then I won't see you too much," I reply. "We'll only move if Mom wins."

"We're moving anyway," Paul says. "If Dad wins his seat again next year."

"Yeah, I'd heard that."

"Well," he says, "better go." He looks at me. "You never did anything about . . . ?"

"No. But the day's not over yet."

"True, but I don't see what you can do now."

"Me neither," I reply.

"Well, bye," he says.

"Bye."

"See you."

"Yeah. See you."

He plunges back into the crowd. I wait a second, then do the same.

And if it looks like Mom is going to lose on the next ballot, to James, he's probably right—what can I do to stop it?

10 P.M.

Mary Strong opens the envelope. She reads. My heart is thumping so loud I can hardly hear. "James" (no that can't be right. James last?) "1,145." A hush falls on the room. Not even the James delegates have the heart to jump up and put on a good face. What's happened? "Green" (Green? Has Mom dropped into second?) "1,703." No, this isn't possible. "Heraux—1,752." The Heraux group goes completely nuts. Then the Green delegates are on their feet. After all there's only fifty votes separating us. Anything could still happen. James's delegates are in a state of shock.

"Well, well, well," Mike says, "so James is the *king maker* now. He'll decide who wins this, Mom or Heraux. He'll have to declare for one or the other of them. Look, here comes one of his aides now to see what kind of deal Mom'll offer him. No doubt he's also got people talking to Heraux."

"What kind of deal?"

"Oh, you know, a cabinet seat, maybe one he'll particularly want."

"Great," I mutter to myself.

James's aides huddle with Mom and her aides for about ten minutes. Mike is allowed to listen on the fringes but I'm forced to sit and watch. Finally the aides leave. Mom actually looks pale. Dad looks distraught. Mike comes and sits back down.

"What? What?" I ask.

"You won't believe this," Mike says, "but James wants Mom to drop out and come to him. He says if she doesn't, he'll go to Heraux who's offered him a very good deal. He says she can have any cabinet post she wants— even finance or external affairs."

"But why should *she* drop out. He's in third. She's in second."

"Right—*second*. He points out she's lost the momentum and he's right. If he goes to Heraux, it's all over."

It's all over, I repeat to myself. I have to act. I have to do something. It's now or never.

I go over to the group around Mom and listen. They are talking fast, trying to decide how to respond to James.

"The thing is," Saul says, "the minute I walk over there, the entire arena will see me make that walk. The James people might assume we're willing to deal before I even get there. Our people will lose confidence."

"We'll send a note," Mom suggests. "With a runner no one will notice. We'll tell him we won't go to him but he can come to us and name his post—*except* finance. I know for a fact Heraux won't go to him, so he'll have to choose."

"You don't want that in writing," Zaida says. "What if a media type gets their hands on it?"

And then I see my chance.

"I'll go," I say, pushing over to Mom.

"What?" she says.

"I'll go." I don't give her time to say no. "I'm perfect. I can take your message, no one'll think anything of me going over there 'cause they'll just figure I want to see Paul."

Mom looks at Zaida. He nods. So do Saul and Cathy.

"Okay, Ali, you've got yourself the job," Mom says. "Now repeat to me what you'll say."

"You want me to tell him that you're not dropping out, but you'd like him to move to you. He can have any ministry he wants outside of finance. Heraux won't go to him either. He'll have to choose between you and Heraux." That's what you want me to tell him, I think. It's not what I *will* tell him though.

"Good girl," Mom smiles. "All right, off you go. There isn't much time."

I begin what feels like the longest walk of my life, over to James's section. He is sitting up high, parallel to us, to our left. I have to go down to the floor, then climb up countless concrete steps until I reach the area where he's sitting. My mind races as I walk. What shall I say to him? I'll finally have a chance to speak and I realize that what I say could change everything. Do I repeat Mom's message as is and leave? And what if he goes to her and she gives him a big cabinet post? And he's discovered? Mom and her whole crowd will look like crooks. But everyone knows that James *hates* Mom. He won't go to her. He'll go to Heraux. Heraux will give him whatever he wants. And Mom will have no power to stop James. If he's caught, they'll all look like crooks. The only way to stop him is to get Mom elected so she can do something. And besides, I admit to myself, I really do want her to win.

So do I add something of my own? Do I follow the small

idea that has been lurking around my brain for the last couple of days? And if I do that, and it works, then what? I might just get my mom elected. Is that what I want? I'd have to move. I swore I'd do anything to avoid that. And yet, it's funny, I can't work up the same horror about the move I felt before I got here. When I look at James and I look at Mom, I realize how important it is that he *not* win. And suddenly, there's Paul, right in front of me.

"What are you doing here?" he asks, looking both bewildered and delighted at the same time.

"I have to talk to your dad. Paul, will you back me up?"

He looks at me and for one brave moment takes my hand in front of all James's top aides, who are staring at me.

"I've done nothing but think about that," he says to me. "I'll have to hear what you say, Ali, and decide then. I'll try to do what's right. That's all I can promise."

"Take me to your leader," I say, squeezing his hand. After all, what more can I expect of him?

I follow him through the gawking masses until we reach his father.

"Dad, this is Ali."

James's eyebrows lift almost to his hairline.

"Hello, Ali."

"Hello, Mr James. Could we talk privately for a moment?"

He kind of grins. "Not now, Ali, I'm rather busy."

"Mr. James, my mom sent me."

"All right, young lady. Follow me."

I follow him up more stairs into a private box. Three aides are with us.

"It has to be private," I insist.

"My aides should hear any deal your mom is offering."

"I don't think so."

He waves them out of the room. He motions me to sit. Paul opens the door and comes in. I take a deep breath.

"Mr. James, the other night when you were in the trailer," I hear Paul kind of gasp, "Paul and I were there, too."

James's face sort of goes rigid. He jerks his head in Paul's direction real fast. You know that expression, "if looks could kill"? Well, if it were true, Paul would be dead.

"We were just talking in the trailer and you walked in, and I guess we panicked. I heard everything."

"So?" he says.

"So," I say, "Mom sent me over here to tell you that you could have any cabinet post you want and that she *won't* go to you. Heraux won't go to you either, so you'll have to choose. That's *her* message. Now this is what *I* want." I feel like I'm choking. What I say here could decide the fate of the entire country and will certainly decide mine! But life is no longer just a simple business of staying in Winnipeg or moving, or people being totally honest or not. If it were I would have just told everything I know to everybody—and hurt Paul and probably accomplished nothing. And now, is what I'm doing right?

"I want you to declare for Mom. I want you to tell her you'll think about a cabinet post after the election and then I want you to refuse it when it's offered."

He's smiling now.

"And if I don't?"

"If you don't, I'll walk straight to the first media type I see and give them the scoop of a lifetime. It'll be on TV in seconds. I overheard you promise the Toronto runway."

Now he's laughing.

"I'm sorry, Ali. I know you're trying to help your Mom. But they won't believe you. They'll think it's a desperate move by a kid who loves her mom a little too much."

143

"They may not believe me on my own," I answer slowly, trying to keep the quiver out of my voice, "but they'll believe Paul and me together. And they'll believe the tape I just happened to have on me at the time."

All the colour drains out of James's face.

"Paul, are you with her on this? Is it true?"

Paul stands there for a minute, not speaking, not moving. Then slowly, he starts to move over to me. When he reaches me he still doesn't speak, but he takes my hand.

"Paul," his dad says, "maybe I was a little hasty, forbidding you to see Ali. But this revenge is a little out of proportion, don't you think? And Ali—if you have such a tape, let's hear it—I want proof!"

"It's not revenge, Dad," Paul says quietly. I can see he's trying real hard not to cry and he's squeezing my hand so hard I think he's going to crack the bones in my fingers. "I don't think you should be prime minister. I wonder now how we got so rich so fast. What you did was wrong."

Before I know what's happening, Paul's father has lunged from his chair and hit Paul across the face. Paul staggers back.

"How dare you!" he screams. "How dare you speak to me that way!"

I grab Paul's hand and pull him towards the door. I shout over my shoulder, "You have ten minutes to declare for Mom before we go to the TV reporters. Ten minutes."

Paul and I rush out of the room. About ten aides are clustered around the door and they practically fall into us when we race out. They try to stop us but we barrel through everyone and head over to Mom's section. The reporters see us and immediately start to gather round us.

"Paul, are you moving over to the Green camp officially, or is this just romance?"

"Paul, is your father going to move?"

"Ali, we saw you go talk to Paul's dad! Any reason for that?"

So much for my idea that no one would notice me. We don't answer anyone. We just try to get through them to the protection of Mom's area, where reporters are kept a reasonable distance away.

"Thanks," I say to him as we clamber up the stairs.

I can see Paul's cheek is getting all red where his dad slapped him.

"You okay?"

He nods but I can see he isn't. That took a lot of guts, what he just did. A lot.

"Took a lot of guts what you just did," he says to me.

"Me? Are you kidding? It's *you* that's got the guts."

"You could've chosen not to say anything," he says. "Or you could've told him to go for Heraux. Your mom would never have known. You could've stayed in Winnipeg like you wanted. And that tape business—what a bluff!"

"I know," I say, feeling slightly ill. The importance of what I've just done makes me feel really queasy.

When we reach Mom, she smiles at us both. Paul puts out his hand for the whole world to see and she takes it and shakes it.

"You didn't have to do that, Paul," she says quietly.

"But I wanted to," he replies.

Oh boy! The TV commentators must be going crazy. Paul James moves to Green! Young love wins out!

Now there is a big kerfuffle going on in the James section.

"What is it?" I say to Paul.

"Dad's moving," he replies. "He's walking. But where?"

Traditionally when a candidate drops out of the race and moves to another candidate, he does just that, literally. He gets up and walks to the person he's going to support,

145

shakes hands for all to see, like Paul just did, and sends out a message to his delegates as to whether he will free them or take them with him. He is moving, but where is he going? No one in our area is speaking, but everywhere around us is pandemonium. My heart is thudding. Will it work? Will he call my bluff? Will Paul and I actually have to go to the media? Would we have the nerve to do it? I steel myself and look at Paul. He nods to me. Yes, we'll do it, if we have to. But how can I ask him to disgrace his father like this? I know it's the right thing to do, but would he ever be able to live with himself after? And if I don't do it, will I be able to live with myself? I look at him and I try to get calm, to think. But it all just keeps going round and round in my head. I could go to the media without Paul, but they wouldn't believe me, James is right about that. So it's together or nothing.

"Paul, Paul," I whisper, "how could you live with yourself, if we did this? He's still your dad."

Paul shakes his head. He has no answer. I start to pray Paul and I don't have to make the decision.

The crowd of media around James must be hundreds thick. He can barely move he is so surrounded by reporters and photographers and camera people. Slowly, slowly, he makes his way down the stairs. Heraux is to the right of us, so James has to go to the right to come to either of us. He's almost at our block of seats now. Any minute he'll turn, come up, shake Mom's hand but no, he's still walking! Jonathan runs up. "He's going to Heraux!" he yells. Everyone groans. "But he's releasing his delegates. There's still hope."

Paul and I look at each other—the moment of decision has come. Have I become like everyone else, can't speak the truth for fear of the consequences?

"I'll do it," he says, but I can see his hands are shaking, just like in the movies.

"No," I hear myself say, "I can't let you. It's not right." I stop for a minute to try to put my muddled thoughts into words. "What your father did wasn't right, but it's also not right for you to humiliate both him and yourself and your whole family. How could you ever live with yourself after that? How could you live knowing you'd destroyed your own dad?"

Paul snorts. "He knew us better than we knew ourselves. He bet that we couldn't do it! Now we'll prove him right."

I sigh. "He could've taken his delegates. The fact he didn't *must* be because of our threat. So we've done something, Paul. Now Mom still has a chance."

Mom interrupts us.

"Ali, Paul, over here. Mike, Terry, get everyone on the floor working. I want every James delegate talked to by one of our people before the next vote. I want everyone down on that floor. Someone get Paul a hat," she commands. A Green hat is placed on his head.

"All right, everybody, get to work. We can still win this one! And especially target the Quebec vote. A lot will now go to Heraux."

We all scatter. Even me. Suddenly I am stopping complete strangers and talking to them as if my life depended on it. I've made my choice and now, more than *anything*, I want Mom to win. I know she's the best. Also, I know that Heraux will make James an important minister and I also know that if Mom wins I'll tell her everything—and I'll bet he won't get what he wants then. Paul is by my side and we're working together on the James youth delegates. He convinces one of the big youth organizers to switch. This guy pulls a lot of weight with the delegates. He and Paul talk

147

to them until one by one they start to take off their James hats and replace them with the piles of Green hats that have suddenly materialized out of Jonathan's hands. Cameramen and photographers and print media surround us constantly and run all over the floor interviewing the converts both to the Heraux camp and to ours. "Who are you voting for? Why have you chosen Heraux? Why have you chosen Green?" The air of excitement and tension has built to an almost unbearable pitch. Paul and I work our way through the crowd, even trying to convince kids as we stand in line to vote. And after the vote we don't stop because what if there is a fourth ballot, so still we walk the floor and try to convert anyone with Heraux hats or T-shirts.

I look at my watch. It's 1:00 A.M. and suddenly I feel like I'm going to fall over.

"Let's go get something to drink," Paul suggests.

I nod and realize that I haven't eaten since that hot dog around 4 P.M.

"Have you eaten today?" I ask Paul.

"Food?" he says, looking puzzled. "I think I've heard of that. A substance that you chew that enables you to live. Right?"

"Right," I grin. "I can barely remember it either," I add.

We make our way through the crowds, the rock and roll still blaring, out to the concession stands.

"How do you feel?" I ask, as we stand in line for our drinks.

"Weird," Paul replies. "Really weird."

"What'll it be like at home?" I ask.

Paul grimaces.

"Exactly the same, I bet. Dad's never around anyway. He'll give me the cold shoulder for a while but that'll probably be it. He won't tell Mom about our little scene, and neither will I, so life'll go on as usual."

I shake my head. I feel really sorry for him, having such a rotten relationship with his dad. I realize that although I resent Mom not being there for me, at least I can respect her for what she does. Paul doesn't even have that. And I respect her a lot more now that I see things aren't always so simple. I understand why she didn't speak out about the rodeo. I still think she was wrong, but I understand better now.

"I wish life were simpler," I say out loud.

Paul sighs. "I wish it were, too. I hope you aren't sorry about what you did," he adds.

"I hope I won't be sorry. You were so great the way you stood up to your dad." I look at his red cheek. "Does it still hurt?"

"Naw. He's never done that before," Paul adds. "I mean he doesn't beat me or anything."

"Good," I say. "He wanted the leadership so bad he'd do anything for it and now he's lost. I almost feel bad for him."

Paul stares at the floor.

"I don't," he says, and I can hear from the bitterness in his voice it'll take him a long time to come to terms with this.

Finally we get our drinks and walk back into the Dome. The chairpersons are standing at the podium!

"Oh my God," I say, and I grab his hand, desperate to get up to Mom and the family before they announce it. But too late. We are half-way up the stairs when Mary Strong opens the envelope and says, "Heraux—2,274. Green—2,325."

And then everything seems to go in slow motion. The crowd around us rising up as one, screaming, "Green, Green, Green!" I drop my drink and it makes a terrible mess as it spills over my sneakers and down the stairs. Two guys in black suits hover over me. Paul puts his arms around my waist, looks into my eyes, and says, "Let's give the newspapers another picture." And he gives me a big kiss right on the mouth.

We turn and make our way up to Mom, who is on her way down to the podium to give her speech. Saul reaches me first. He gives me a peck on the cheek and says, "Damn shame it's not in prime time."

Mom comes next. I give her a big hug. She hugs me back and continues down. And then it hits me. I turn to Mike who is by my side and he picks me up and gives me a huge bear hug.

"We won, we won!"

And I let out a big whoop as I feel him crush the air out of me.

"We won!" Mike puts me down. "Come on, we have to go on stage." Dad comes up and takes my hand.

Paul waves to me as I turn to go with my family.

"See you in Ottawa," he calls.

"Yeah," I call back. "See you in Ottawa."

"Write?" he yells.

"For sure," I scream back.

And then clutching my dad's hand, I follow my family onto the stage, to the wild cheering of the crowd.

TUESDAY, SEPTEMBER 2
(TWO MONTHS LATER)

7 A.M.

I'm getting dressed for my first day at my new school in Ottawa. I'm nervous and I hope I don't get treated too differently because of my Mom. Stornoway, the official opposition leader's house, is pretty fancy but Mom says not to get too comfortable—we'll be moving in the spring right after the election, into the P.M.'s residence. If the polls are to be believed, she's right too.

I told her about James's deal. At first she was furious that I'd kept it secret. Then she got busy trying to figure out how to handle him. It was a real problem, because she couldn't afford to lose all his supporters just before a general election, which is what would happen if she didn't give him a good post in her shadow cabinet. (That's what they call the cabinet when it's in opposition.) She thought of leaking it all to the newspapers but that would tarnish the whole party and create a scandal just before the election.

So she called him in to her office one day and had it out with him. She told him he'd be Health and Welfare critic until the election. After the election, he would have a cabinet post, not necessarily that one, on one condition—the bureaucrat in charge of the department would answer directly to her as well as to him. That way, no under-the-table deals were possible as she would scrutinize everything. He agreed. This way Mom keeps the party together, keeps James honest, and keeps an eye on him. I would've like to see him fired but it's not so simple. As I discovered this summer, nothing ever is. Still, Mom thinks he might get sick of having such a tight rein on him and decide to give up politics and go back to business. I hope she's right.

So Paul will move here in the spring if his dad wins and we'll probably go to the same school. We write all the time and he's come down for the day a few times over the summer on his own, and for two weeks he stayed at his dad's flat, while his dad was away in Europe. His mom came too and I met her. She's nice. I like her.

Things with his dad turned out just as Paul had predicted. His dad was very cold to him, but he couldn't vent all his anger at Paul without Paul's mother finding out about what had happened. Things soon returned to normal between them—normal being that they hardly ever spoke and hardly ever saw one another.

Paul and I just get closer and closer. I feel pretty lucky to have met him. This whole thing worked out lots better than I'd thought it would.

In fact, I sometimes find myself going to Question Period on Parliament Hill just to see Mom and her colleagues in action. I can see that what they're doing is very important and affects every part of our lives. And sometimes I sit in on those meetings she always invites me to—and I actually am starting to find them interesting. I keep telling Mom that I'm going into science not politics. She says that's great but it won't save me from making tough choices that'll affect people's lives. I've certainly learned that making these choices can be horribly difficult. Still, Mom always says one person can make a difference and in this case that person was me. Had I not confronted James, he might have taken all his delegates to Heraux and he'd soon be a minister who could give away goodies under the table. She says I did something and I should be proud of it. It did work out but what if James had completely called our bluff and taken all his delegates with him? Then how would my decision look now? Not very good, that's for sure.

I sigh and try to make my stupid hair do something. This T-shirt is no good, I'll have to change again. Then I can't help but smile to myself. Deciding which T-shirt to wear should be a piece of cake after the decisions I had to make this summer.

So why isn't it? Which *should* it be—the blue or the black?

About the Author

Carol Matas is the author of many juvenile novels, including *Lisa*, named a *New York Times* Notable Book of the Year and a 1991 Young Adults' Choice by the International Reading Association. Both *Lisa* and its sequel, *Jesper*, were honoured by the Canadian Children's Book Centre as Memorable Books for Young People in 1990.

Carol Matas lives in Winnipeg with her husband, Per Brask, and their two children.